Study Guide

Audio Adventure - Volume 3

Table of Contents

Episode #25 – *The Winds of Change - Part I* **7**

Romans 1:23

Lightening Storms.....*7*
Fulgurites.....*8*
New Age Religions.....*9*

First Teaching of New Age.....*9*
Second Teaching of New Age.....*10*
New Age and Design.....*11*

Episode #26 – *The Winds of Change - Part II* **13**

Hebrews 11:6

Punctuated Equilibrium.....*13*
Using the Evidence to Investigate
   the Fossil Record.....*16*
Chaos Theory.....*19*

Let's do Some Chaos Experiments!.....*20*
Is the God of the Bible Like
   the New Age Force?.....*23*
Affects of New Age.....*24*
New Age Crossword.....*25*

Episode #27 – *The Eye of the Storm - Part I* **27**

Genesis 7:11

Differences Between Tornados and
   Hurricanes.....*27*
Tornados.....*28*
Hurricanes.....*30*
The Largest Storm of All: Noah's Flood.....*34*

What Would Cause the Oceans
   to be Warmer?.....*34*
Creation Model for the Flood.....*35*
Computer Modeling of Hypercanes.....*36*

Episode #28 – *The Eye of the Storm - Part II* **37**

Job 38:22-29

Power of the Worldwide Flood.....*37*
The Ice Age.....*40*
What Caused the Ice Age?.....*42*

Ice Cores.....*43*
Does the Bible say Anything About an
   Ice Age?.....*44*
The Power of God.....*45*

Episode #29 – *The Temple of the Moon - Part I* **46**

Gen 11:1-9

Anthropology.....*46*
Where did all the Languages of the
    World Come From?.....*47*
Exploring Genetic Traits.....*48*

Let's Look More Closely at Language.....*51*
Languages Have Changed Over Time *52*
Language Problems for Evolution.....*54*
The Evidence Fits with the
    Biblical Account *54*

Episode #30 – *The Temple of the Moon - Part II* **55**

Genesis 1:27

How Does Evolution Explain Language?.....*55*
There are Important Differences Between
    Ape and Human Communication.....*57*

Humans Designed for Language.....*58*
Tower of Babel legends.....*62*

Episode #31 – *The Midnight Prowler* **64**

Matthew 24:37-39

Nautiloids.....*65*
Evolutionary Story *67*
How Are They Found in the Rocks?.....*68*

Fossil Heads! Yes Heads!.....*69*
Was the Grand Canyon Formed by
    the Worldwide Flood?.....*71*

Episode #32 – *Destination Moon - Part I* **72**

Psalm 97:6

Beautiful Stars.....*72*
What is the Evolutionary Story?.....*73*
Modern Nebular Hypothesis-the Evolution
    of Our Solar System.....*75*

Purpose of the Moon.....*78*
Moon Phases.....*80*
Earth's Stability.....*81*

Episode #33 – *Destination Moon - Part II* **82**

Psalm 33:6

Gravity.....*82*
The Other Planets.....*84*

The Earth is Unique among
   All the Planets.....*85*

Episode #34 – *Destination Moon - Part III* **89**

Psalm 148:4-6

Earth's Moon.....*89*
The Race to the Moon.....*92*
Moon Dust.....*96*

Life on the Moon?.....*97*
The Apollo Hoax.....*98*
Nothing Left to Chance.....*100*

Episode #35 – *The Wilderness Express - Part I* **101**

Genesis 1:21-25

Created Kinds.....*101*
Unfossilized Dinosaur Parts?.....*102*

Variation in Animals.....*104*
Design of a Snowflake.....*107*

Episode #36 – *The Wilderness Express - Part II* **109**

Jeremiah 27:5

The Life of a Salmon.....*109*
Polar Bears.....*112*
Caribou.....*113*

Porcupine.....*114*
Man's Best Friend-Dogs.....*115*
Wilderness Express Crossword
   Puzzle.....*118*

Getting the Most From This Study Guide

The Jonathan Park Audio Adventures were produced to help children and families have a strong foundation in which to build their faith! Unfortunately many live as if their belief in the Bible is just another brand of religion. However, God has given us a gift that we often take for granted – He has asked us to believe in truth! Sadly, many Christians are intimidated by evolutionary ideas and told that the Word of God has been disproven by science. The truth is that if God really created the universe, animals, and mankind like He said in Genesis, we should be able to investigate this world and find evidence that what He says is true… and we do!

Think about the difference between the Christian and evolutionary worldviews. If evolution is true, then there is no God and we are the product of random evolutionary processes. As nothing more than a bunch of molecules, we have no purpose in life. On the other hand, if we were created, it means that we were made especially by a loving Creator who has a unique purpose for each of our lives! This difference can completely change a person's life! Truly knowing that God's Word is true is a foundation that will change every aspect of a child's life. That's what we hope to accomplish with the Jonathan Park project – to teach families about scientific evidence that is in harmony with God's Word.

We've designed the audio adventures so families can enjoy them in their cars – while on trips or just running errands. They can listen at home or during family devotional time. Our goal is to provide exciting adventures that run deep with creation apologetics and Biblical lessons. We hope that you enjoy them regardless of where you listen to them!

This Jonathan Park Study Guide has been designed to maximize teaching from each episode in the Jonathan Park Series. Our hope is that after listening to each Jonathan Park Audio Adventure, parents will sit down with their children and work through the information provided in this booklet. Here's how we recommend you use this guide with your child:

1. Listen to an episode from the Jonathan Park: The Winds of Change – Album #3.
2. Begin your study by praying with your child. Pray that God will teach you truth and continue to build your faith.
3. In the Table of Contents, we've listed Scripture references for each episode. Spend time

reading through this section of God's Word.

4. Next, open this Study Guide to the corresponding section. The information is arranged in bite-sized nuggets – each builds upon the previous one. Read through the information with your child and relate it back to the Word of God.

5. Let the child ask questions, and help them find answers. This Study Guide may be the key to unlocking doubts that a child has. Always follow up a child's question. Refer to other creation science resources, or make a commitment to search for the answer together. These questions are excellent ways to take them deeper into God's Word.

6. End in prayer. Thank the Lord for the specific things He has taught during this time.

While this Study Guide is designed to address *scientific* issues, we have also created devotionals that focus on the *Biblical* aspect of the topics presented on each episode of Jonathan Park. In addition, we have also prepared Real Adventures – activities that can be used to reinforce the information within this booklet. For these devotionals and activities, go to www.JonathanPark.com and click on "Real Adventures".

"But sanctify the Lord God in your hearts: and be ready always to give an answer to every man that asketh you a reason of the hope that is in you with meekness and fear."

- I Peter 3:15

Lightning Storms

Have you ever been caught in a lightning storm? It can be a very exciting and hair-raising event! If you are close to a storm your hair really will stand up!

Do you know what you should do if you are caught in a lightning storm?

Use the 30-30 rule, count the time until you hear thunder. If that time is 30 seconds or less, the storm is within 6 miles of you.

Seek shelter such as a large permanent building, ditches, trenches or low ground. Place yourself in a low crouching position with feet together and hands over ears. After the last flash and bang it is best to wait 30 minutes before leaving your safe place.

Flash to bang count

5 seconds = 1 miles
10 seconds = 2 miles
20 seconds = 4 miles
30 seconds = 6 miles

WARNING

DO NOT go near metal, water, under trees, on hills, or near electrical equipment.

Fulgurites

Lightning is very hot and, as the boys discovered in this episode, when it hits the ground, under the right circumstances, it can make formations called fulgurites.

There are two types of fulgurites -- sand fulgurites and rock fulgurites.

The sand fulgurite is the most common. When lightning strikes sand a tube-like structure is formed by the sand being melted together.

A rock fulgurite forms when lightning strikes a solid rock and creates a surface coating of glass around the rock. Wow, lightning is amazing!

Many religions around the world believe that some objects have special powers. The new age movement believes that fulgurites and crystals have these powers.

New Age Religions

There are many religious ideas around the world. It is important to be aware of what some of them are:

- Hinduism originated in India.

- Taoism began in China by a man named Lao-Tse in 604-517 BC.

- Buddhism was started in India by a man named Gautama in 563-480 BC.

- Confucianism originated in China by a man named Confucius in 551-479 BC.

New Age philosophy has taken ideas from these religion's ideas, and others, and combined them into a modern religious philosophy.

Two teachings of the New Age are:

New Age philosophy

- Truth is determined by what we *feel* to be right.
- Evolution is assumed to be true -- that humans have evolved from animals. They believe that we are now continuing to evolve spiritually.

Let's look at the first teaching of new age.

"Truth is determined by what we feel to be right. Something becomes real if we believe it to be true."

Do you know where truth comes from? Where right and wrong comes from? Truth comes directly from God's Word. Not from what we might think or feel is true.

Psalm 146: 5-6 "⁵*Happy is he that hath the God of Jacob for his help, whose hope is in the LORD his God:* ⁶*Which made heaven, and earth, the sea, and all that therein is: which keepeth <u>truth for ever</u>*"

Feelings should not be more important that God's word. It is important to remember that feelings are REAL -- God made us emotional beings, but our feelings are not always RIGHT. God's Word and character help us know what is right.

Let's look at the second teaching of the New Age movement:
They see the evolutionary process like this:

Big Bang

galaxies and planets

life on planets

animals evolving into people

conscious evolution of humans

spiritual evolution of humans

New Age teaches that evolution has really happened. They believe that over billions of years the universe was created, including galaxies, planets, and life. They also believe that animals have evolved into humans.

Next, they believe that humans evolved to be conscious. That means the earth has evolved human beings that <u>know</u> that they are evolving. Remember how new age teaches that something becomes true when someone believes it to be true? That's why *some* New Agers believe that evolution had to make humans that were conscious of the earth so that it could be real!

New Age teaches that we are entering a very special time in evolutionary history. They believe that we are beginning to evolve spiritually, and that someday we will become new spiritual beings. They do not know what this would actually mean because no one has 'arrived' at this level. However, they believe that it might be a "universal consciousness" - which means that we will all think as one -- and that all life throughout the universe would finally live in peace.

New Age and Design

The New Age movement acknowledges that the universe is designed. They recognize how complex life is, but deny that the God of the Bible is the Creator.

Romans 1:18 & 19 says *"18For the wrath of God is revealed from heaven against all ungodliness and unrighteousness of men, who hold the truth in unrighteousness; 19Because that which may be known of God is manifest in them; for God hath shewed it unto them."*

This verse says that people suppress, push away, or deny the truth-even though the truth has been shown to them. They choose to deny truth. New Age philosophy is like this. They see the design of the universe but choose to suppress the truth of God as the Creator.

Look at the table below. You can see the differences between New Age and what the Bible teaches:

New Age	Bible
Nature is creator	God is the Creator
Nature is divine	God is divine
Earth is evolving itself (Gaia)	God guides and sustains the earth
Universe evolving itself (Anthropic)	God upholds the universe and set it all in motion.

Notice the two words in the table in parenthesis. The two words are "Gaia" and "Anthropic". Have you ever heard the phrase "mother earth"? This phrase comes from the Gaia hypothesis that says the *earth* is evolving itself -- like it has a mind of its own. The Anthropic Principle is the idea that the *universe* is also evolving itself.

Answer the following questions using the table above:

1. What is creator in the New Age movement?

   _____

2. Who is Creator according to the Bible?

   _____

3. Read Romans 1:20-23. Does the new age idea fit this description?

   _____

4. List one way that new age and Christianity are opposite:

   _____

Punctuated Equilibrium

Do you remember how evolution is supposed to have happened?

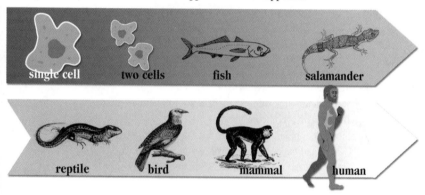

single cell   two cells   fish   salamander

reptile   bird   mammal   human

The general idea is that simple things evolve gradually first and then more complex things evolve from that. A single cell is thought to be simple and a human is thought to be very complex.

If a single cell evolved into a human over millions of years, it should have left lots of evidence behind. However, there is no **evidence** to support this gradual model of evolution left-over in the fossil record!

Do you know what **evidence** is? Evidence are facts that support an idea.

Evidence

Practice your skills using evidence with the following puzzles:

**Who's Driving
the Cars?**

Three cars: one yellow, one red, and one blue-were driving on the road early this
morning. Read the following pieces of evidence. Can you tell the color and type of
each car, who is in each car, and which country the people come from?

People	Kind of Car	Country	Color
George	Sedan	France	Blue
Inez	Sports Car	Italy	Red
Marcy	Truck	Sweden	Yellow

List of evidence
1. Marcy is not in a yellow car and is not from France.
2. The red car is not from Italy
3. Inez is in a blue car but she is not from Italy or Sweden.
4. George and his dog are in a truck with an Italian flag.
5. The sports car is from France, while the sedan is red.

A chart may help you organize the evidence.

	Kind of Car	Country	Color
George			
Marcy			
Inez			

Using the evidence, did you figure out the color and type of each car, who is in each
car, and which country the people come from?

Answer:

	Kind of Car	Country	Color
George	Truck	Italy	Yellow
Marcy	Sedan	Sweden	Red
Inez	Sports car	France	Blue

14

Who's Telling the Truth?

Three kids left footprints in the school cafeteria. All three wear the same type and size shoes so the janitor could not tell which kids left the prints. Julie said "I didn't do it." Crissa said "William did it." William said "Crissa is lying." Only one of the friends is telling the truth and the other two are lying. Whose prints are on the floor?

If you need help, use the table to find the answer:

If William did it	True or False
Crissa's statement is	True
Julie's statement is	True
William's statement is	False

If Crissa did it	True or False
Crissa's statement is	False
Julie's statement is	True
William's statement is	True

If Julie did it	True or False
Crissa's statement is	False
Julie's statement is	False
William's statement is	True

> Remember only one friend's statement can be true.

Answer:
The footprints are Julie's. As we can see in the tables above, that is the only case in which only one friend's statement is true.

15

Using the **Evidence** to Investigate the Fossil Record

Just like we solved these puzzles, we can look at the evidence as we try to understand the truth about evolution. When we look at the evidence of the fossil record what do we find?

List of facts	What Evolution Would Expect
Whole, fully formed plants & animals	Incomplete plants & animals still evolving
No transitional fossils - bones of one animal turning into the other	Bones of animals that are half of one type of animal, and half of another
Complex and simple things found together in the same layers of rocks	Simple things at the bottom of of the fossil record, complex at the top – simple and complex would not be found in the same layers

This evidence does not support evolution.

Because people choose not to acknowledge God as Creator - that He created animals fully formed from the start, they must make another explanation for the evidence. Because there are no partially evolved animals or plants in the fossil record, they have devised a fairly new idea called 'punctuated equilibrium'.

New Age has incorporated this model into their beliefs.

! ` ? ; ' . " , ( )
Punctuation

You are familiar with the word 'punctuation'. At the end of a sentence, for example, is a period. A period tells you the end of a thought and the beginning of a new thought or sentence.

The punctuation in the punctuated equilibrium theory is like a period - it is the end of one type of animal, and the beginning of something new.

There is a sudden amazing appearance of one complete animal in the fossil record. Then there is another appearance of another type.
– see the period?

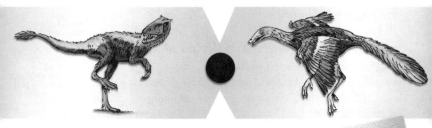

– Some believe there was a punctuation (quick change) as one animal turned into another.

Punctuated Equilibrium claims that this evolutionary change happened so fast that it didn't have time to leave evidence in the fossil record.

Equilibrium

You are familiar with the word 'equal'. Equilibrium is very similar. It is like the balancing of a teeter totter - it doesn't move, and just stays in the same place without moving. The weight on either side must be equal. Then it is said to be in equilibrium.

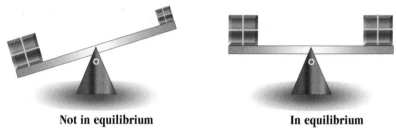

Not in equilibrium   **In equilibrium**

The equilibrium (no changes) in the fossil record is seen as the evidence that there is no change in the animals for long periods of time. They are balanced. They appear in the fossil record fully formed and complete. And this is what we actually *do* see – the fossil record shows no sign of one type of animal changing into another. Everything seems to stay the same.

Quick Changes Followed by a Period of No Change

In summary, punctuated equilibrium means that evolution happens in spurts followed by long periods of no change, and then suddenly more quick changes, again followed by no change.

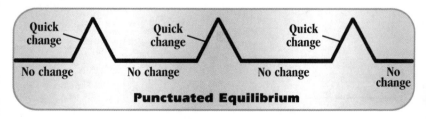

This is why many New Agers like this theory - they believe the quick changes were being controlled by the "mystical force" that is creating all life.

However, there is a big problem with punctuated equilibrium. They say that evolution is true because there's no evidence of it in the fossil record because it happened too quickly. That would be like saying, "elephants must run through our houses very fast because we never see them."

If the evidence shows that there weren't changes happening in the fossil record, a better explanation would be that changes weren't happening at all - not that they were too quick to see! God's Word has a better explanation: God created animals fully formed from the beginning.

I am trying to prove this CHAOS THEORY!

Chaos Theory

"This house is CHAOTIC!"

Has your mother ever made a comment about the house being messy and chaotic? Does she mean that the house was clean and orderly, or dirty and out of order?

Chaos Theory is the study of things that are too complicated to precisely predict like the weather or other seemingly random events.

In order to predict something we look for patterns. Do you know what a pattern is? See if you can find the patterns below.

Circle the repeating pattern.

FROGFROGFLYFROGFROGFLYFROGFROGFLY

Fill in the next part of the pattern.

2 4 6 8 ___   1 2 3 5 8 13 21 34 ___

These are examples of patterns. Once you have figured out the pattern you can use this understanding to predict the next outcome.

Even in things that appear random, we can usually find patterns.

Let's do some chaos experiments!

Wooden Top Experiment

Materials:

Wooden top   Large smooth surface   Good observation skills

Find an old fashioned wooden top. Locate a smooth, flat surface to spin your top. A floor or a table top works well. Make sure there is enough room for the top to spin with out running into things. Spin the top. Carefully watch the patterns that the top makes as it spins. Spin the top at least ten times. Even though the pattern made by the top seemed very chaotic, did you observe it repeating any parts of patterns as it spun? If yes, this is an example of 'patterns (or order) found in chaos.' If not, spin the top until you do (it will eventually repeat similar patterns for a moment before embarking back onto a chaotic path).

Splatter Experiment

Materials:

3 colors of tempera paints

Old toothbrush

White paper

Procedure:

Mix the tempera paints so that they are watercolor consistency. Place them in three separate bowls. Dip the bristles of the toothbrush into one color. Tap off excess paint so that it does not drip on its own. Place the brush over the white piece of paper and splatter the bristles using your finger or by tapping the brush across your finger. Notice the marks on the paper. Repeat this procedure for each color of paint. Try to start your splatter in the same location each time.

Even though the paint seems to randomly fall to the paper, do you see any repeating or similar patterns in the spatter marks? This is an example of 'order' found in chaos.

Rain Drop Experiment

Materials:

Black piece of construction paper

Procedure:

If it is raining outside, take the piece of construction paper outside in an open area and set it on level ground. Observe how the raindrops fall on the paper. Do any raindrops fall in the same places? If yes, this is an example of 'order' found in Chaos.

Conclusions

You can see from the experiments that some order can be observed from random events. Is this order enough to make anything? Some evolutionists believe that an explosion (known as the big bang) blasted all the material -- to make the universe -- outward. This explosion caused a huge mass of chaos that they believe eventually formed patterns. Their theory says that those patterns eventually became solar systems, planets, and caused life!

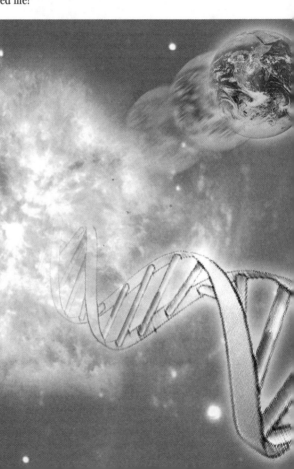

Do you think that the chaos made by the big bang explosion could form an orderly pattern of planets, our solar system, the balance of nature, and complex human bodies? **NO!**

It is impossible for an explosion to create the great order that we see in our world. Use your imagination to picture a disorganized junkyard. Could an explosion in the junkyard assemble a car? Could that explosion create order out of the chaos? **NO!**

What's the big deal?

New Age philosophy likes Chaos Theory. Since they understand that it would be impossible for an explosion to create all of this order by itself, they claim there's a mystical force that has guided the chaos.

This is an erroneous conclusion! Do you know what erroneous means? It means in error or wrong.

The big deal is that the Big Bang has not been proven by science to have happened, evolution has not been close to proven, and there is not evidence for a mysterious cosmic force as described by New Age philosophy.

Maybe a better conclusion for the order that we see in our universe is to say that the world was made by the Creator!

Is the God of the Bible Like the New Age Force?

Is believing that a cosmic force evolved the universe, the same as believing that a Creator made the universe? No. They are very different teachings, but only one can be true. Let's look at the evidence:

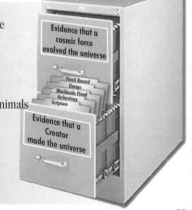

Evidence that a cosmic force evolved the universe

0

Evidence that a Creator made the universe

1. Fossil record shows fully formed plants and animals
2. Evidence for design
3. Evidence of a worldwide flood
4. Archeology confirms the history of the Bible
5. Scripture in harmony with science

Not everything has a scientific explanation:

We say that there is no scientific evidence for their belief, but couldn't they say the same thing about the Bible when it talks of miracles?

Actually the scientific evidence is in total harmony with the Scriptures. When God performs miracles it is clear that God is stepping outside His laws in order to accomplish his will, to show His superiority over nature.

Think about the account of creation itself. The Creator supernaturally made the entire universe out of nothing! Yet, the scientific evidence left behind seems to show that this miracle really did take place. That's what we'd expect if God's account was real. It would be consistent with the physical laws of the real world - but show His power to rise above the natural!

Even though our faith is not a blind faith (as other religions), it is built on the truth. Yet we still come to Him by faith:

Hebrews 11:6 says *"⁶But without faith it is impossible to please him: for he that cometh to God must believe that he is, and that he is a rewarder of them that diligently seek him."*

Affects of New Age

Be aware of how New Age philosophy may affect you.

Three of its core teachings:
Truth is determined by feelings instead of facts
Nature is God
We are gods (this is the original sin of Genesis)

All of these ideas are the opposite of the truth we learn in God's Word.
Romans 1:25, *"²⁵Who changed the truth of God into a lie, and worshipped and served the creature more than the Creator, who is blessed for ever. Amen."*

Remember that God is the author and creator of all things so we are responsible to Him. As we obey and love Him, He loves us, and keeps us in His care!

New Age Crossword

Across

5. A group of facts supporting an idea.
6. Scientists use this to find evidence about the past.
8. These happen when God steps outside the laws of physics.
10. A random theory that New Age uses to support its beliefs.

Down

1. A lack of evidence is the reason for this theory. Punctuated _____.
2. An old religion.
3. It is a combination of old religions and new ideas.
4. New Age acknowledges that the universe is _____.
6. A formation made by lightening.
7. In error.
9. God is the _____.

Solution to crossword

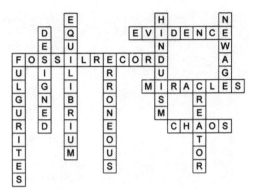

Part 1

Differences Between Tornados and Hurricanes

Do you remember the most severe storm that you have ever experienced?
What did the clouds look like?
How was the air moving?
Was there rain or thunder?
How much damage did it do?

There are many types of storms all of which have things in common such as the water cycle, cloud formation, and wind. Some storms form over land, and others form over water. Tornados and hurricanes may be two familiar storms to you.

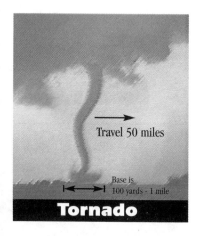

Travel 50 miles

Base is 100 yards - 1 mile

Tornado

Travel 500 miles

100 miles

Tropical water

Hurricane

Tornado qualities

Formation: form over land
Size: base 100yds to over a mile
Duration: as long as 50 miles
Wind Speeds: 40 - 318 miles per hour
Forward Speed: 0-60 miles per hour

Hurricane qualities

Formation: over warm tropical oceans
Size: up to a few 100 miles across
Duration: can travel 500 miles
Wind Speeds: 74 to more than 155 miles per hour.
Forward Speed: 10-20 miles per hour over the ocean

Tornados

Tornados come from energy released in a thunderstorm. This energy is concentrated in a small area. In the United States, tornados form East of the Rocky Mountains to West of the Appalachian Mountains. They also occur in Australia and Europe. Tornados occur in the Spring and Summer seasons usually in the late afternoon or evening when the temperature is just right.

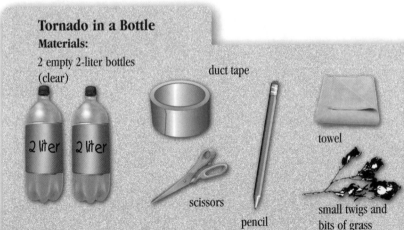

Tornado in a Bottle
Materials:

2 empty 2-liter bottles (clear)

duct tape

towel

scissors

pencil

small twigs and bits of grass

1 2 liter

2

3

4 2 liter

Procedure:

1. Cover the mouth of one bottle with a strip of duct tape. Press tape to the bottle securely.
2. Punch a hole in the tape with the pencil, making the hole slightly larger than the pencil.
3. Fill the other bottle half way with water. Add some small twigs and grass.
4. Put the taped mouth of the empty bottle on top of the mouth of the other bottle. Use several pieces of duct tape to tightly secure the necks of the two bottles together.
5. Quickly flip the bottles over. Grab the taped necks firmly with one hand and swirl them in a circular motion parallel to the floor. Set them down on a table and observe the results.

Tornado Chasers

There are people who track tornados during the storm season. They have special equipment such as cameras, anemometers (measures wind speed), and other instruments that help them gather information about the storm. These people have a dangerous job -- or for some -- it is just a hobby, but they must know what to do if they are caught in the danger zone!

Jokes

What ever happened to the cow that was lifted up into the air by the tornado?

Udder disaster!

Did you know that hurricanes have names?

Each hurricane season, the World Meteorological Organization names the hurricanes that form. There are six lists of male and female names ordered alphabetically. The first hurricane of the season gets a name that begins with the letter 'A' and so on. There are two different lists of names one for the Atlantic and another for the Eastern Pacific. The name lists are recycled every six years. If a hurricane does significant damage its name is retired and replaced.

How are Hurricanes made?

Hurricanes usually form when the ocean temperatures are hotter than 80 degrees Fahrenheit. Basically if there is cloud growth near the equator, it may form a low pressure region. The low pressure will draw in air and vapor from very long distances. It will begin to spin as a result of the Coriolis Force.

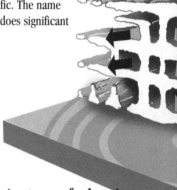

Anatomy of a hurricanes

The Coriolis Force

Imagine if you took a cup of water, and placed it on a pottery wheel. As it spun around and around, the water would also begin to whirl around in a circle inside the cup. In a similar way, because the earth is spinning, storms also begin to rotate.

The **Coriolis Force** is a force that deflects moving objects to one side because of the rotation of the earth.

As the air moves toward the center of the low pressure region, it speeds up like an ice skater drawing in their arms and spinning faster and faster. In the center of the storm an "eye" forms where the winds are calm - and there aren't any clouds. Around this eye forms a wall of clouds called the eyewall. This wall is made of rising air that produces clouds that condense liquid water. This process releases more heat, which causes the air in the hurricane to expand -- lowering the pressure even more. This draws in even a greater amount of air and vapor from the ocean surface from even further distances. If the hurricane lasts for several days or weeks it can become very intense.

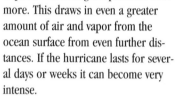

So it becomes a huge heat engine, drawing in air and vapor from far away, shooting it up the eyewall, and ejecting it out the top of the storm, only to cycle it around again.

The earth rotates once in a 24 hour period. That is how we get our day and night. The earth is tilted to its side as it rotates. Hurricanes that form in the Northern hemisphere (North or above the equator) rotate clockwise and hurricanes that form in the Southern hemisphere (South or below the equator) rotate counterclockwise. This rotation is because of the Coriolis Force.

Cloud in a Bottle

Let's look at how a cloud might form over the ocean with a simple experiment!

Materials:

Clear jar   Hot water   Ice cubes   Strainer

Procedure:
Fill the jar completely with hot water for about a minute.
Pour out all the water except for about an inch.
Put the strainer over the top of the jar.
Place three or four ice cubes in the strainer.
Observe.

Explanation: The cold air created by the ice cubes collides with the warm moist air in the bottle causing the water in the air to condense and form a cloud.

Cloud formation is one of the steps needed in forming a hurricane. You just experienced the beginning steps of a tropical storm! As the clouds form into thunderstorms in the ocean, they bunch up and begin to rotate because of the Coriolis Force.

Jokes

What did one hurricane say to the other?

I have my eye on you!

Saffir-Simpson Scale

Category 1-5	Wind speeds	Damage
1	74-95 miles per hour	Minor
2	96-110 miles per hour	Pulls off pieces of roofs
3	111-130 miles per hour	Structural, flooding
4	131-155 miles per hour	Rip apart roofs, destroy mobile homes, massive flooding
5	155 mph and over	Destruction of houses and other buildings, severe flooding

Believe it or not, even more powerful hurricanes may have existed in the past. It is called a hypercane. Hypercanes where first proposed in the 1990's by a man named Kerry Emanuel.

Hurricanes are fueled by ocean temperatures that are at least 80 degrees. What if the oceans where 40 degrees Fahrenheit more than that? There is good scientific evidence to show that might have been the case. This would produce hypercanes with wind speeds exceeding 300 miles per hour!

Look at the table above to answer the following questions.

Which category of hurricane has wind speeds of 111-130mph?

The highest wind speed is from what type of hurricane?

How many times faster would a hypercane's wind speeds be compared to a category 5 hurricane?

During the flood, there may have been:

Hypercanes   **Rain**

Volcanoes   **Wind**

Earthquakes   **Warming oceans**

Now that's a powerful storm!!

If the oceans were warmer in the past, it may give Creation Scientists clues to the flood, and how hypercanes might have played a part. If the oceans were warmer, this gives the fuel needed - heat -- to make bigger and more damaging storms.

What would cause the oceans to be warmer?

In Genesis 7:11, it mentions "the fountains of the great deep" opening up. This is a clue to what was happening during the first part of Noah's flood. This may mean that there was volcanic activity in the bottom of the ocean. The waters near this hot lava would be significantly warmed.

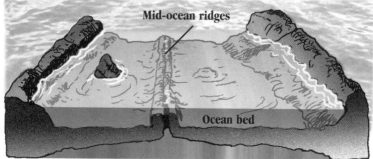

There is a 4,000-mile long chain of mountains on the bottom of the ocean called the mid-ocean ridges. These enormous mountains may have been formed during the flood and been the site for some of the volcanic activity during the flood.

Creation Model for the Flood

Some creation scientists have modeled what they believe was happening during the flood. First imagine the earth's surface made up of plates. No, not dinner plates! More like the cracked shell of a hardboiled egg, notice the graphic. The cracks are the edges of the plates on the earth. Next, one of these plates begins to sink down into the outer layer of the earth. As it sinks, it causes friction, which in turn produces more heat - making the plate sink even faster (like pushing a hot knife through butter). This action has a fancy name called Thermal Runaway Subduction. As the hot plate and lava underneath meet the cool ocean water, it sends bursts of super-heated steam plumes of water up into the atmosphere. The water eventually falls back to the earth as rain which may have supplied the earth with "forty days" of rain as the Bible states. This would also be good conditions for the formation of hypercanes!!

super-heated steam

Earth plate sinks

Is there any scientific evidence for warmer oceans?

Yes, there is.

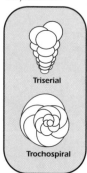

Triserial

Trochospiral

The evidence is found in cores that scientists have drilled from the ocean floor. These cores have been found to have little marine fossils in them called *Benthonic foraminifera*. They are small marine animals (protozoa). Benthic means bottom dwelling. They secrete or make their own shell made of calcium.

In their bodies these fossils have two types of oxygen called ^{18}O and ^{16}O. By comparing the amounts of each of these, scientists can estimate the temperature of the ocean at the time they became fossils. Scientists have found evidence of higher temperatures in the past.

By placing the cores in the context of a Biblical age for the earth (6,000 to 10,000 years old), the data shows that there is a large increase in temperature-possibly more than 40 degrees, just a few thousand years ago! It appears that there was an event that suddenly raised the temperature, and then the oceans slowly cooled down to what we have today. *This evidence is what creation scientists need to support their idea!*

Computer modeling of Hypercanes

In 1988, NASA collected lots of data from a hurricane named Florence which was in the Gulf of Mexico. They used it to do a study of hurricane behavior.

NASA allowed the Institute for Creation Research to use the data to run their own simulations. However, ICR changed one thing. Do you remember what is needed for a hypercane to happen?

On their model, ICR changed the starting ocean temperature to 35 degrees hotter and then ran the computer model. Eighteen hours into the simulation, Florence became a hypercane! Its wind speeds were over 440 mph and its size covered most of the Gulf of Mexico, and it gave off ten times more rain!

This computer modeling helps creation scientists to test their ideas and give support to the Biblical account of Noah's flood.

Part 2

Power of the Worldwide Flood

In the boxes below, is a list of evidence for the worldwide flood -- which testifies to the power that must have been present to make the things we see on the surface of the earth today.

From the description of the evidence, match the picture with the description by placing the appropriate letter in the space provided.

A

Water deposited sediment
(rock layers)
Sediment is
-moved long distances
-in the US some sediment layers
stretch over several states

B

Bent sediment layers
-in the Peruvian Andes limestone
has been bent with great force

C

Ayers Rock in Australia
-5 miles around, nearly 4 miles
from its base to its top
-made from sedimentary rock
deposited by water

D

Dinosaur National Monument
-we find dinosaurs, clams, snails,
logs, and wood pieces buried
together by volcanic and flood
activity

E

Grand Canyon
-animals called nautaloids were
killed and buried very fast and are
found in one layer in the canyon

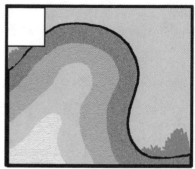

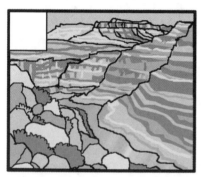

All of these evidences have one thing in common – water played a major part in their formation!

Test your knowledge!

Tornados form over _____.

Hurricanes form over _____.

Hypercane wind speeds are _____ than hurricane wind speeds.

What type of storm may have dropped lots of rain during Noah's flood?

What important condition was needed in the ocean to form a hypercane?

What may have caused warmer oceans in the past?

What are benthonic foraminifera?

What evidence do creation scientists use to support the flood?

How is Dinosaur National Monument evidence of the power of a world-wide flood?

The Ice Age

The Ice Age sometimes seems mysterious or strange. Often you see pictures of those hairy elephants known as wooly mammoths frozen in time, ice caves, "cave men" carrying sticks, or maybe even saber toothed tigers.

Let's try to put the Ice Age into a Biblical framework and talk about the scientific evidence.

Do you know the answers to the following questions?

Q: What does the Ice Age have to do with Noah's flood?
A: The conditions after the flood may have made an Ice Age possible.

Q: What is the Ice Age?
A: It is like a really long winter.

Q: When did the Ice Age happen?
A: Possibly soon after Noah's flood.

The BIG PICTURE of the Ice Age

The story of the Ice Age has two sides, the evolutionary side and the creation side.

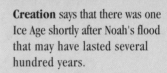

Evolution says that there were several Ice Ages over millions of years.

Creation says that there was one Ice Age shortly after Noah's flood that may have lasted several hundred years.

Misconceptions:

Ice never covered all the land on the earth. Only 1/3 at the most.

All the animals and people did not die, though some may have gone extinct, many moved and adapted to other areas.

What Caused the Ice Age

How did the Ice Age happen? Our theory begins with warmer oceans and cooler continents.

We have talked about how the volcanic activity may have warmed the oceans but how would the continents become cooler? If there was volcanic activity during the flood, there would be lots of "aerosols" (volcanic dust) in the air. These particles would reflect the sunlight back into space making the continents colder.

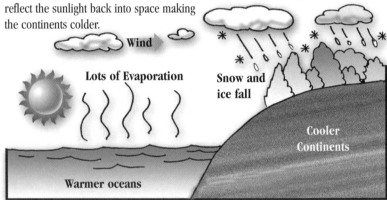

Warm oceans would cause lots of evaporation, and wind currents would carry the moisture to the poles. Because of cooler continents, the moisture in the air would condense and fall as snow and ice.

This idea has been confirmed by another computer model simulation.
The Institute for Creation Research used a computer program made by the National Center for Atmospheric Research to see if an Ice Age would develop under certain given conditions -- mainly warmer oceans and cooler continents.

They found that it would cause large amounts of rain and snow along the edges of the continents and at the poles. Because of this, and other models, creation scientists believe that there were ice sheets that formed quickly in Greenland, Antarctica, and North America. This Ice Age may have lasted for several hundred years after the flood.

Ice Cores

Evidence has been gathered about the Ice Age from ice cores in Antarctica and Greenland. There is that word again -- 'cores'. Ice cores are drilled deep into the ice like a tree core is taken from a tree. Have you ever seen a tree core? It has layers of yearly growth rings where you can see wet and dry seasons, and you can count the age of the tree.

Ice cores can show similar information. Ice cores have layers that can be interpreted as yearly snowfall layers -- made from summer and winter seasons.

A well known core, called the Vostok Ice Core, was collected in East Antarctica by a Russian expedition. It is 6,249 feet long (2,083 meters). That is almost 1000 feet longer than a mile!

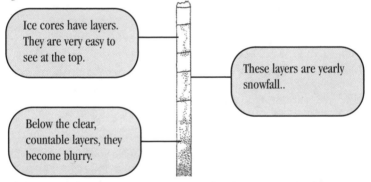

Ice cores have layers. They are very easy to see at the top.

These layers are yearly snowfall..

Below the clear, countable layers, they become blurry.

Evolution

Evolutionary scientists keep counting down into the blurry layers. They add them up to thousands of years of snow fall.

Creation

Creation scientists say that the blurry layers are not yearly snowfalls but many snow storms during one season. These many snow deposits would have been caused by hypercanes over a short period of time.

Creation calls for a short amount of time because of Biblical history and evolution calls for a large amount of time because it demands it. As you can see from our two boxes, the time-frame can completely change the interpretation of the ice core. But it's exciting to see that the ice core may be providing evidence for a hypercane model during the flood.

Does the Bible say anything about an Ice Age?

The Bible does not specifically mention an Ice Age, like it does about the worldwide flood. However, we do know from physical evidence on the earth that it seems that parts were covered with large amounts of ice for a period of time. Job, a relative of Shem, who was Noah's son, lived not too long after the flood. He may have lived during the Ice Age. Look at the following verses from Job:

Job 6:16 *"16Which are blackish by reason of the ice, and wherein the snow is hid:"*

Job 9:30 *"30If I wash myself with snow water, and make my hands never so clean;"*

Job 24:7 *"They cause the naked to lodge without clothing, that they have no covering in the cold."*

Job 24:19 *"19Drought and heat consume the snow waters: so doth the grave those which have sinned."*

Job 37:6 *"6For he saith to the snow, Be thou on the earth; likewise to the small rain, and to the great rain of his strength."*

Job 37:9 *"9Out of the south cometh the whirlwind: and cold out of the north."*

Job 38:22 *"Hast thou entered into the treasures of the snow? or hast thou seen the treasures of the hail,"*

Job 38:29 *"29Out of whose womb came the ice? and the hoary frost of heaven, who hath gendered it?"*

How many times is the word snow used?

How many times is the word ice used?

In what verse is both snow and ice used?

There are still large glaciers that exist on the earth -- besides the permanent ice found in Alaska, Greenland, and Antarctica. In Canada, there are several ice fields. One glacier called the Athabaskan Glacier is found on the Columbia ice fields. You can take a bus tour out on to the glacier, walk around on it, and even have a drink of the pure, cold, icy glacier water!

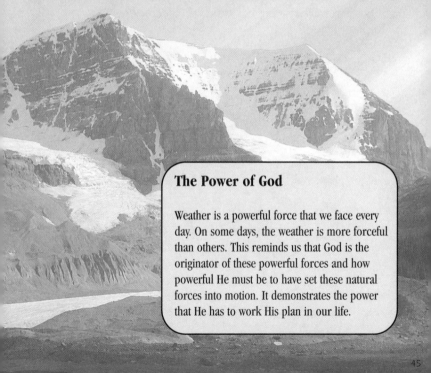

The Power of God

Weather is a powerful force that we face every day. On some days, the weather is more forceful than others. This reminds us that God is the originator of these powerful forces and how powerful He must be to have set these natural forces into motion. It demonstrates the power that He has to work His plan in our life.

Part 1

Anthropology

Anthropology is the study of human nature, human society, and human past. Anthropologists try to make a picture of a people's way of life and bring together social, religious, economic, political, and linguistic parts.

Cultural anthropology, biological anthropology, linguistic anthropology, and archaeology are all parts of the general field of anthropology.

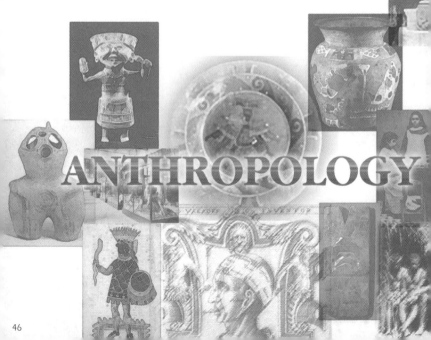

Where did all the languages of the world come from?

The Bible gives us the answer to this question.

Gen 11:1-9 - "*¹And the whole earth was of one language, and of one speech.*

²And it came to pass, as they journeyed from the east, that they found a plain in the land of Shinar; and they dwelt there.

³And they said one to another, Go to, let us make brick, and burn them thoroughly. And they had brick for stone, and slime had they for morter.

⁴And they said, Go to, let us build us a city and a tower, whose top may reach unto heaven; and let us make us a name, lest we be scattered abroad upon the face of the whole earth.

⁵And the LORD came down to see the city and the tower, which the children of men builded.

⁶And the LORD said, Behold, the people is one, and they have all one language; and this they begin to do: and now nothing will be restrained from them, which they have imagined to do.

⁷Go to, let us go down, and there confound their language, that they may not understand one another's speech.

⁸So the LORD scattered them abroad from thence upon the face of all the earth: and they left off to build the city.

⁹Therefore is the name of it called Babel; because the LORD did there confound the language of all the earth: and from thence did the LORD scatter them abroad upon the face of all the earth."

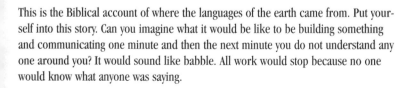

This is the Biblical account of where the languages of the earth came from. Put yourself into this story. Can you imagine what it would be like to be building something and communicating one minute and then the next minute you do not understand any one around you? It would sound like babble. All work would stop because no one would know what anyone was saying.

At Babel, not only were languages born, but also nations and cultures. Many believe that family groups would have spoken the same language. Because they could not understand other family groups, they decided to move away and find their own place to live. They would have scattered throughout the earth.

Families isolated from others would begin to show their own unique genetic traits. A genetic trait is like your eye color or shape of face or whether or not you can curl your tongue. Your genes decide what you are going to look like.

Exploring genetic traits

What color are your parents', brothers', or sisters' eyes? Fill out the chart using abbreviations such as 'b' for blue and 'B' for brown and 'g' for green.

Person	Eye color
Mother	
Father	
Sister(s)	
Brother(s)	
Yourself	

What color of eyes does most of your family have?

This is the prominent eye-color trait in your family. Brown eye color is dominate over blue eye color. The 'B' (brown) overshadows the color 'b' (blue). However, if all of your entire family has blue eyes, then the blue eye color trait has become the prominent color. If you marry a person who has blue eyes and you have blue eyes, then your children will also have blue eyes.

Brown eye color is dominate over blue.

Let's look at another genetic trait -- ear lobes. The dominate ear lobe structure is the kind that is unattached or free to flop. The other type is attached.

Fill in the chart for your family with 'F' for free and 'f' for attached:

Person	Ear lobe type
Mother	
Father	
Sister(s)	
Brother(s)	
Yourself	

Attached   **Unattached**
                      Free to Flop

Which trait did most of your family have?

Let's do one more genetic trait, tongue curling. Do your family members have the ability to curl their tongue as they stick it out? Believe it or not, this is a genetic trait!

Fill in the chart using 'T' for no tongue curling and 't' for tongue curling:

Person	Tongue curl?
Mother	
Father	
Sister(s)	
Brother(s)	
Yourself	

No tongue curling   **Tongue curling**

Which trait is most present in your family?

How does a tongue curl relate to nations of the world?

In a small population, such as a family, it is easy to see that certain traits can become more common than others. This is similar to how nations and cultures were formed as family language groups moved away from Babel and became isolated from other groups. As the families grew and inbred, distinctive characteristics of skin color, height, hair texture, facial features, temperament and other characteristics became known as the traits of nations or tribes that we have today.

This is how we can some-times distinguish between groups of people and nations -- by their appearance. Norwegians typically have fair skin, blonde hair, and light colored eyes. Asians typically have dark straight hair, dark eyes, and medium colored skin. East Africans typically have dark curly hair, dark skin, and dark eyes.

These nations have come to look a certain way because their family group migrated away from Babel toward their own area of the world. And because they stuck togeth-er, they shared common traits, and their appearance resembled each other.

Let's look more closely at language.

There are over 6,000 distinct languages that can be traced back to a few older language stocks. It is difficult for those who study languages to find the original family stock. Linguists look for similarities among the languages to find a common origin. Look at the following examples:

Germanic	
English	Water
German	Wasser
Danish	Vand

Slavic	
Russian	Voda
Polish	Woda
Czech	Voda

You can see that the word for 'water' is very similar in each group, but when you look at Germanic and compare it with Slavic it is not so similar.

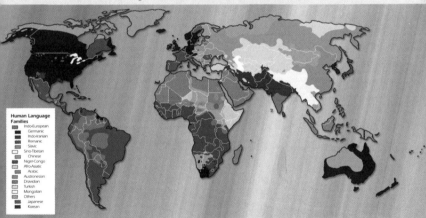

Human Language
Families
- Indo-European
- Germanic
- Indo-Iranian
- Romanic
- Slavic
- Sino-Tibetan
- Chinese
- Niger-Congo
- Afro-Asiatic
- Arabic
- Austronesian
- Dravidian
- Turkish
- Mongolian
- Others
- Japanese
- Korean

95% of the world speaks only 13 different languages. The languages are:

Mandarin Chinese	**Bengali**	**Korean**
English	**Portuguese**	**Hindi**
Malay-Indonesian	**Spanish**	**French**
Russian	**Japanese**	**Arabic**
German		

This writing is an example of Arabic writing. Some of you may have never seen Arabic before. It is a beautiful script and appears rather complicated to our eyes.

Decrease in Complexity

By themselves, languages tend to deteriorate.

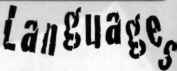

Think about what's been happening to English over the last 200 years. People just naturally simplify the way they say things.

Think about the word "you" in our modern English. A long time ago, if you wanted to call a person - you would have used the words "thou" or "thee". If you wanted to call a group of people, you would have used the words "ye" or "you". We have dropped these older words from how we speak today.

Old English was used about 600 - 1100 AD. English is a Germanic language from the Indo European stock. Some Old English and Modern English words are listed below:

Old English

gaers
blioe, glaed
cirice
hlaefdige
lufian, lufu
modor

Modern English Translation

grass
happy
house of worship
lady
love
mother

You can see how much English has changed over time. How do you think that it might change in the future?

52

Increase in Complexity

While some words or grammar has been lost, other words have been added. For example, English has increased its vocabulary by adding words needed to communicate about technology. The words 'cell phone' and 'web site' were not in our vocabulary until a few years ago. Most Americans only use 800 to 1000 words in everyday conversation. A college student at graduation knows about 20,000-30,000 words, which are less than 2% of all English words!!

Languages also borrow words from other languages increasing their vocabulary and their complexity.

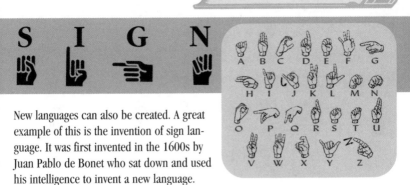

New languages can also be created. A great example of this is the invention of sign language. It was first invented in the 1600s by Juan Pablo de Bonet who sat down and used his intelligence to invent a new language.

The general rule for languages is that they'll usually deteriorate when left alone – but they can increase when words are borrowed, or when a group of people invest energy and a plan to construct language rules or make new words. Overall, some linguists agree that the addition of language, and the deterioration of language, has resulted in equilibrium -- the level of complexity has remained the same and consistent.

Language Problems for Evolution

Over history, it looks as if the level of complexity in language has remained the same and consistent. It seems that languages can change into other languages, but human language as a whole never becomes more complex.

This causes a problem for evolution. Since language does not increase in complexity, but stays the same, how could language evolve from nothing to the complex languages we have today? That's more possible proof that languages were complex from the very start, and that fits well with the Tower of Babel account.

The Evidence Fits with the Biblical Account

Another thing that linguists have found is that languages can change into others very rapidly. This also fits the Genesis account -- that there were several language stocks created during Babel and that they adapted into the thousands of languages that we have today.

Part 2

How Does Evolution Explain Language?

Evolutionists think that language had to evolve from our animal ancestors. There are several theories about how this might have happened:

Bow Wow	Anomynopedic (This means that the sound of the word resembles what it means.)
Yo ee hoe	Grunts that helped people coordinate group efforts
Marxist	Animal gestures evolved into speech
Polygenesis Theory	Many languages evolved at the same time (Because apes may have evolved into humans in more than one place they each invented their own language.)
Psychedelic Glossolalia Hypothesis	The idea that prehistoric man started eating fungi that gave them hallucinations, so they started uttering new sounds that eventually evolved into language.

None of these theories even come close to explaining how man began speaking with grammar – able to communicate complex ideas. Language not only communicates everything our senses can taste, touch, smell, see and hear, but it also allows us to express very complex concepts like love, hate, and jealousy. And that fits best with the idea that language was given to man by their Creator!

Humans Learn Language in Two Ways:

Acquisition	Learning
is the natural way a child aquires their first language.	is the studying, reading, practicing, and memorization of a language.

What do you think are some differences between humans and animals?

Animals can communicate with each other in limited ways, but we have the unique ability of speech. There are ways that we are "Made in God's image" – our ability for speech, relationship with God, and amazing creativity certainly sets us apart from the animals. Though animals are valuable, it is important to understand that as humankind 'made in God's image' we are God's special creation, more special than any animal. God made our value real by dying for us on the cross.

Genesis 1:27 says, "*27So God created man in his own image, in the image of God created he him; male and female created he them.*"

There are Important Differences Between Ape and Humans Communication.

For humans, hearing is more important than sight for communication. For apes, sight is more important than hearing for communication.

Animals do not have the biological structures for speech. They lack such things as the tongue and the palate.

Interestingly, Toto, a famous African gray parrot in England, sounds very human because it can pronounce words very clearly. Like humans, birds can produce complex sounds. Birds and humans share a layered system that uses tunes and dialects which are controlled by the left side of the brain. Like children, young birds have a stage called 'sub-song' which resembles the babbling of a young child. But Toto does not have a 'language' as we understand it.

A child that is five or six years old can use over 16,000 words.

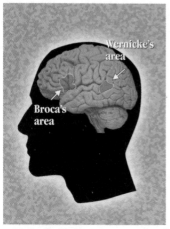

Humans Designed for Language

It has been discovered that certain parts of the brain have been designed for language. These two areas on the left side of the brain were discovered by a couple of doctors who had patients with brain damage.

Broca's area in the left hemisphere of the brain is known for the formation of speech. Wernicke's area is known as a place where language is understood.

Obviously the brain is essential in forming and understanding language. Also, other anatomical parts for producing speech are primarily found in humans rather than any other animal. God has specially designed our voice box.

Only humans can produce what is known as speech. Surely this is part of what makes humans 'in His image'.

This is a drawing of the vocal structures found in the throat of a human. These structures along with our lungs, mouth, lips, tongue, and brain enable us to form words. All of these structures must be fully functioning and in place in order for language to be formed.

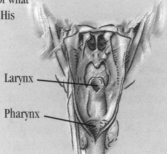

How could the random chance of evolution produce ALL of these necessary structures all at once?

How to Play Exploring Ancient Ruins.

Find a token around the house that will represent you as a player, something small such as a bean, nut, or even a dime. Up to four players can play at a time.

Place your tokens at the Start space on the game.

Roll a six-sided number cube to see who goes first. The person with the highest number starts. Roll the number cube at the beginning of each turn to decide the number of squares to move.

Take turns in a clockwise direction. Each person follows the directions on the space in which they land.

WINNER

The winner is the player who reaches the Finish space first. *Congratulations!* You have successfully completed your first Anthropological Expedition.

To set the scene of the game, imagine being a person named C. Leonard Woolley and team. They discovered and excavated the Royal Tombs of Ur. Ur is known as the birthplace of Abraham of the Bible.

They found 1800 burial sites, 16 of which they think were of royal people. The royal tomb of Queen Puabi was found untouched. The tomb had a chamber set at the bottom of a deep "death pit". Her name is known by a seal found on her body written in Sumerian, one of the oldest written languages.

Board spaces:

27
28
26 Translating a tablet. Move ahead to 28.
25 Car trouble again. Move back to 22.
24
29 Lost direction again. Move back to 24.
30 FINISH
START
Lea and lang Mov
1 Off to a slow start.
6 Car trouble. Move to 1.
Hospital
2
3 Learn a language. Move to 5.
4 Snake Bite. Go back to hospital.
5

Genesis 11:31 says, *"And Terah took Abram his son, and Lot the son of Haran his son's son, and Sarai his daughter-in-law, his son Abram's wife; and they went forth with them from Ur of the Chaldees, to go into the land of Canaan"*

10

12
Found a burial ground. Move to 12.

13
Found pottery. Move to 14.

14

9

Wrong direction. Go back to 10.

WRONG

16
Found a tunnel to the tomb. Move to 20.

Found a tunnel to the temple. Move to 27.

17
Lost direction. Move back to 12.

22

21
Found precious stones. Move to 24.

20

19
Discover scrolls supporting Bible. Move to 22.

18
Skip a turn to find directions.

Queen Puabi wore a headdress of gold leaves and ribbons, lapis and carnelian beads, gold chokers, necklaces and earrings. She was covered in strings of beads made of precious metals and semi-precious stones and had rings on all her fingers.

Many cultures throughout the world have legends in their history that give an account of the story of the flood and the tower of Babel. The island of Hao, an island in Polynesia, has a story about the tower of Babel and a god coming, breaking down the building and making them have diverse languages. This story was passed down by their ancestors long before European missionaries could have shared the story with them.

A Chaldean legend says that the inhabitants of the earth were proud of their own strength and size and began to build a tower. God sent wind that ruined the tower and introduced a diversity of languages -- they had spoken the same language before.

Quiche Mayas have a sacred book that narrates the story of Babel.

Indian (Kaska) peoples have an account called 'History of Berosus' by Abydenus that locates Babel at Babylon on the banks of the Euphrates river.

The Sumerian epic "Enmerkar and the Lord of Aratta" also gives an account similar to the happenings at the tower of Babel.

These other accounts of Babel may be shadows from the true account recorded in Genesis. As the people spread out and began their own nations, they possibly would tell the story

in their own languages and cultures. Over time, those stories would begin to change a little, and some of the specifics would be lost, but the basic story would be similar. The Tower of Babel was a real event - and now peoples from all around the world have those stories left-over from their past.

The ancient seas had many creatures that we still have today and many others that have gone extinct. On the whole, our modern seas don't have the vast variety recorded in the fossil record. That is hard to imagine by looking at the abundance we see now.

Early Ocean Scene

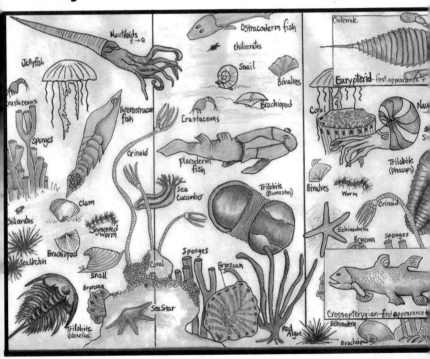

Nautiloids

Nautilus are part of a group called invertebrates. Invertebrates are animals that have no skeleton, but often have a protective covering like an exoskeleton or a shell.

Invertebrates usually live in the shallow part of the ocean near the Inter-Tidal Zone - the place where the ocean tides move up and down, exposing areas at low tides and covering them at high tides.

Nautilus are living today in our oceans.

Nautiloids are only found as fossils (some up to 3 feet long).

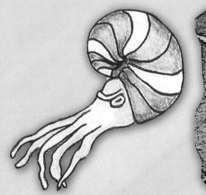

Coiled nautilus

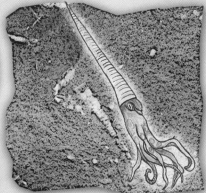

Straight shelled nautiloid

A nautiloid's body resembles that of a squid. It has six tentacles that reach out from the end of the shell which has 15-20 chambers inside. Most likely they would have swum in a motion similar to the nautilus that lives today.

Make Your Own Nautiloid Model

Materials:

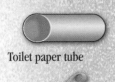

Toilet paper tube

Piece of notebook paper

Scissors

Markers

Procedure:

Cut the piece of paper into 6 strips that are about a quarter of an inch wide and 6-8 inches long. Crease the toilet paper tube on both sides (by pressing it flat just a little bit). Now cut along the creases, up to about an inch of one end. Now roll-up the opposite end so that it makes a cone. Glue it in place. Next glue the ends of the 6 strips of paper equally spaced around the inside of the large opening of the tube. These are the legs of the Nautiloid. Draw lines around the body of the nautiloid, adding the texture of the shell. Lastly, stuff the tube with tissue paper. Let some stick out of the opening with the tentacles and put two large dots on the paper for eyes.

Nautiloid fossils, unlike live nautilus, are only found as the mineralized shell. The soft body parts, like the legs, are gone.

How are Nautiloids Fossilized?

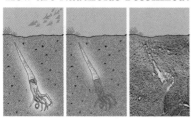

- the animal is first buried
- the heavy mud or sand that buried the animal kills the creature
- the quick burial often keeps the animal parts together, free from scavengers
- the soft parts rot away
- the hard parts become like rock by absorbing minerals from the mud.

The Redwall Limestone is a rock layer that stretches from Arizona to Utah. Creation scientists believe the size of this deposit is a testimony to the catastrophic forces of the worldwide flood. A special part of this layer is a six-foot-thick section called the Whitmore Nautiloid bed found in the Grand Canyon, and this is where we find the nautiloids.

Evolutionary Story

They say that the Redwall limestone was formed *gradually* over *very long periods of time.* They believe the area was originally an ancient sea. As Nautiloids died *over time*, they would sink to the bottom and be buried by limestone as it also *gradually* settled.

Can you pick out the key words of this story? (hint: they are italicized)

What is different about this theory from the process of fossilizing nautiloids that we discussed earlier?

If the Nautiloids died gradually over a long time, they would all rot away or be eaten by scavengers before they could become a fossil.

They had to be buried quickly not gradually.

There are billions of baby (small) and adult (large) nautiloids found through out the Redwall layer, and they are buried in a pattern.

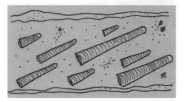

Observe the picture on the left, can you see the pattern?

Many of the fossils all appear to be facing in the same direction. This is called non-random distribution. It is like the game of Pick-Up-Sticks. When you gather the sticks according to the rules, and let them fall, they fall in a random manner, but if you cheat and make them all fall in straight rows, this is non-random.

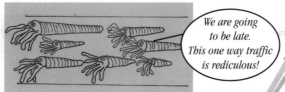

We are going to be late. This one way traffic is rediculous!

This evidence indicates an underwater avalanche called a *sediment gravity flow* came through and quickly buried all things in its path. The fossils face the direction that the avalanche was traveling and nautiloids where washed to their burial place and became fossils.

If the evolutionary story was true and the nautiloids were dieing gradually of old age, why would we find old fossils and young ones buried together? All of this is evidence of a large-scale catastrophe. Could it have been Noah's Flood?

Fossil Heads! Yes Heads!

Well, we are not talking about regular heads from humans or a cat, but fossil coral heads. Corals are invertebrates like nautiloids. There are soft corals, like sea fans, and hard corals, like brain corals. Hard corals group themselves into colonies called coral heads.

A coral is a little animal, though you may think that they look like plants. The little animal is called a polyp.

Coral has an opening that takes in food and gets rid of waste. It has six or more tentacles that collect its food. It makes its own home out of calcium carbonate, into which it retreats during the day, or for protection.

Coral reefs are made by huge numbers of these polyps that have formed into coral heads. All of the polyps in a coral head are connected by their tissue. They share their food with each other. If one polyp eats, all of the polyps eat too!

These coral heads are also found as fossils in the Redwall limestone layer -- along with the nautiloids. Each coral head is about the size of a football, and they appear to have been picked up and moved to their burial place just like the nautiloids.

Density Experiment

Materials:

Clear bottle and lid

Small rocks

Toothpicks

Muddy water

Procedure: Fill the jar full with muddy water, but not so muddy that you can't see through the water. Put about five small rocks in the jar - these will represent the coral heads. Now, add about ten toothpicks. These represent nautiloids. Put the lid on tightly.

Make a prediction: When shaken up, will the coral heads, the nautiloids, or both be at the bottom, top, or middle of the jar? Why?

Shake the jar.

Result: You should find the heavier more dense coral heads at the bottom of the jar and the lighter less dense nautiloids near the top of the water.

How are coral heads and nautiloids buried in the Redwall limestone?
Interestingly, they are not buried as you would expect based on our experiment. It looks like fast moving, muddy currents picked up both the nautiloids and the coral heads and buried them together! It would take violent water action to cause this to happen! It definitely was not gradual slow movement.

This would mean evidence for a worldwide catastrophe - like a flood that covered the entire earth. Coral heads and nautiloids are supporting evidence!

Was the Grand Canyon Formed by the Worldwide Flood?

How could the flood both lay down the layers, and cut through those very same layers at the same time to form the canyon?

Many people do not have a good answer for this question. The rock formation that we have been talking about, the Redwall limestone is found as one of the layers in the Grand Canyon. There is good evidence that Noah's flood was responsible for laying down these layers.

There is evidence that the soft sediment layers had time to harden awhile before the canyon was carved out. If those layers didn't have time to harden after being deposited by the flood, the flood waters would have made them droop and slide down like mashed potatoes. This would mean that the original flood event could not have both laid down the layers AND carved out the canyon at the same time.

The conclusion:
Something other that Noah's flood may be responsible for making the Grand Canyon.

So What Cut the Canyon?
Scientists have found evidence that there might have been several lakes that formed sometime after Noah's flood. There were natural dams that held huge amounts of water -- possibly as big as Lake Michigan. When the dams eventually broke, all of the water would have suddenly been released with enough force to carve the Grand Canyon very rapidly.

Part 1

Beautiful Stars

Psalm 97:6 - "6The heavens declare his righteousness, and all the people see his glory."

Wow, what a wonderful clear night! Look at how many stars you can see. On a dark clear night your eyes can see about 3000 stars. Star gazing can be a pretty fun activity. Have you ever tried to identify constellations? Constellations are the groups of stars that you can see at night. Some that you many be familiar with have names like Orion, Big Dipper, Little Dipper, and Cassiopeia (looks like a sideways "W"). Stars are gaseous balls of hydrogen and helium.

Did you know that there are about 10^{22} stars in the universe?
That is 10,000,000,000,000,000,000,000 stars.

It is true that the heavens declare the glory of God.

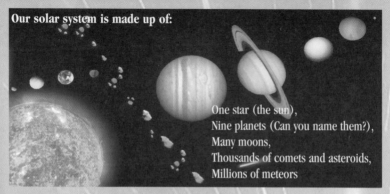

Our solar system is made up of:

One star (the sun),
Nine planets (Can you name them?),
Many moons,
Thousands of comets and asteroids,
Millions of meteors

The distance across (diameter) of our solar system is over 7 billion miles.

Psalm 33:6 says, *"By the word of the LORD were the heavens made; and all the host of them by the breath of his mouth."* God's Word plays an important part in His creative process. He simply spoke and called things into existence.

What is the Evolutionary Story?

According to evolution, our solar system formed through the process of the Big Bang. The Big Bang began with the explosion of a small "kernel" of mass energy about 15 million years ago. As things spread out from this explosion, they cooled and formed hydrogen and helium atoms. Then about 10 million years ago, the first stars began to form and eventually made galaxies like ours -- the Milky Way.

Our solar system began with a gas cloud that condensed down into the sun. Some theories say the sun's strong gravity captured planets that were traveling past. Other theories say that the sun pulled material away from other stars, and that it eventually formed planets and moons as they began rotating around our sun.

73

What is Wrong With the Evolutionary Story?

What are the problems with the evolutionary story about the formation of the Solar System?

• Gas clouds in space normally *expand* or spread out instead of *grouping together* to form planets.

• Planets and moons orbit around the sun in a delicate balance of circular orbits. Physics teaches us that objects moving away from an explosion (like the big bang) would either continue traveling in a straight line or crash into the sun, pulled by its gravity. So where did the circular orbits come from?

So, one reason that the evolutionary theory falls short is that it cannot explain the formation of the planets in the first place. Secondly, even if planets could have formed, physics shows us that it would have been impossible for them to begin orbiting the sun.

Planetary Orbits

An orbit is the path that heavenly bodies such as planets and moons travel around another.

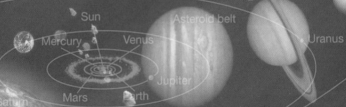

Stability is provided by the fact that all objects in our solar system orbit the sun. The entire Milky Way galaxy also has a circular rotation.

Modern Nebular Hypothesis-the Evolution of Our Solar System

This idea is similar to the ones discussed earlier. In this theory, we start with a huge spiraling ball-shape of dust and gas. As gravity begins to pull material toward the center, the ball begins to flatten out into a disk shape. As more matter gets pulled into the center, it begins to form the sun. The gas and dust in the outer parts of the disk eventually lump into the planets and moons.

The problems with this idea have to do with two principles of physics -- *angular momentum* and *distribution of mass*.

Angular momentum measures an object's tendency to continue to spin. The way its mass changes affects its motion -- this is called the *distribution of mass*.

First let's look at ordinary momentum.

You have experienced momentum when you ride your bicycle. Momentum is the tendency of an object to stay moving along a straight path. This is why you need breaks on your bike -- your momentum will keep you moving. This is also why we need seatbelts in our cars, when the car stops, our bodies keep going. The belts stop our momentum.

Which do you think has more momentum?

A bus moving at 15mph or a bicyclist moving at 15mph?
(hint: what is the difference between a bus and a bicyclist?)

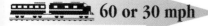

A train moving at 60mph or the same train moving at 30mph?

The bus has more momentum than the bicyclist because it has more mass (it is heavier) even though they are traveling at the same speed. The train moving at 60mph has more momentum because it is traveling at a faster speed.

With ordinary momentum mass and speed are two important factors.

Here are some illustrations of angular momentum and how mass affects the spinning motion:

Ice Skater – Have you ever seen an ice skating competition? An ice skater experiences the interactions between mass, and movement. To spin faster, the skater brings their arms and legs in close to their body. To slow down the skater holds out their arms or legs. It takes lots of practice and experience to be able to control the spinning movement.

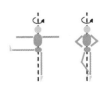

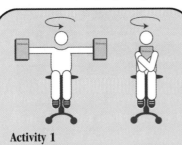

Activity 1

Swivel Chair – If there is a swivel chair in your home, you can demonstrate this principle. Sit down with a large book such as a dictionary in each hand. Have someone spin you in the chair. Hold out the books as far as you can. Then bring them back in close to your body again. You should experience a dramatic change in the speed at which you are spinning.

By moving the heavy dictionaries, you are moving your mass in and out, and this changes your spinning motion.

Activity 2

Merry-go-round – Have several of your family members ride on a merry-go-round. First have them all stand or sit in the center as you begin spinning them. Next, have them all move out towards the edges of the merry-go-round (you are redistributing the mass). The merry-go-round will slow down. If they move to the center again, it will speed up.

Summary

You can see from these activities that angular momentum is affected by speed and mass of objects -- and the distance from the center of their orbit.

These two principles of angular momentum and distribution of mass, show that the Modern Nebular Hypothesis cannot be true.

The problem

Remember that the Nebular hypothesis says that a gas cloud contracted because of gravity, and then the sun, moons, and planets formed from the disk-shaped cloud?

Because it is at the center, and because it weighs more than the planets and moons, the sun should be spinning faster than the planets.

We know this because of angular momentum and the distribution of mass just as the ice skater illustrated. The body of the ice skater represented the sun in the center, and the arms represented the planets and moons.

The sun has such a large mass it should be rotating very fast - it makes up 99% of the material in the solar system, and yet the planets and moons actually have 99% of the movement. This is exactly the opposite of what we should see if the Modern Nebular Hypothesis were true.

The problem is that we currently observe that the sun rotates slowly compared to the planets and moons. The observable facts and the theory contradict each other -- so the theory is false.

Purpose of the moon

Genesis 1:16-19, *"And God made two great lights; the greater light to rule the day, and the lesser light to rule the night: he made the stars also. And God set them in the firmament of the heaven to give light upon the earth, and to rule over the day and over the night, and to divide the light from the darkness: and God saw that it was good. And the evening and the morning were the fourth day."*

From this verse, it is obvious that God made the moon to give light upon the earth during the night time. Interestingly, the moon has no light of its own. The composition of the rocks and dust of the moon are just right for reflecting the sun's light back to the earth. This is a good analogy for how we are designed to reflect the Son of God's light to the people around us. It says in Mathew that we are the light of the world and not to hide your light. We are to let it shine so that all men can see it and praise God because of it.

The sizes of the moon and sun are also designed:
- The moon is 400 times smaller than the sun.
- The sun is 400 times farther away from the earth than the moon is away from the earth.

These two facts mean that from the earth, the moon and the sun appear to be the same size. This proportion allows the sun to be blocked out by the moon when their orbits cross paths. This is what we call a solar eclipse.

Make a Scale Model

Materials:

Butcher paper

Scissors

Ruler

Pencil

Compass

String

Tape

Procedure:

To make scale models of the earth moon and sun, we have to shrink the diameters of each object using the same scale (The scale used here is 1.9 x 10-9). The diameters are already figured out for you.

Sun diameter- 2.7 meters
Earth diameter- 2.5 centimeters
Moon diameter- 0.68 centimeters

Using a ruler, mark the diameter of the earth and the moon on a piece of paper with a pencil and compass draw the two circles using the measurements as the diameters. Tape several pieces of butcher paper together so that you can measure, and mark the diameter of the sun. Cut a piece of string that is half the size of the sun's diameter (1.35 meters) and place one end of it in the center. Tie the other end of the string to a pencil. Stretch out the string and carefully draw a circle (It may be necessary for two people to help). Cut out each circle that represents the sun, moon, and earth and compare their sizes relative to each other.

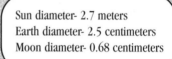

Did you know that the sun was that big compared to the earth?
Did you know that the moon was that small compared to the sun?

79

Moon Phases

The moon cycle marks our months of the year. It moves through the following phases once about every 29 1/2 days.

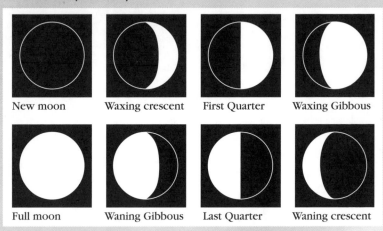

New moon   Waxing crescent   First Quarter   Waxing Gibbous

Full moon   Waning Gibbous   Last Quarter   Waning crescent

You may have heard the phrase 'once in a blue moon' which usually means 'almost never'. A blue moon is what we call it when there are two full moons in one month. A blue moon happens only about 7 times in 19 years.

Has the moon ever really turned blue?

There have been a few times when the moon has appeared to be blue.

• In 1883, an Indonesian volcano (Karakatoa), exploded. The volcanic material in the atmosphere turned the sunset green and the moon blue.

• In 1927, the monsoon season was very late in India. Winds blew dust from the dry ground into the air and turned the moon blue.

• In 1951, a huge forest fire in Western Canada sent particles up into the air. From the Northeast United States it looked like a blue moon.

As the diagram shows, the center axis of the earth is not straight up and down but slanted. The earth sits in space at a 23 degree axis tilt. Our moon's gravitational pull and orbit helps to stabilize this tilt.

Scientists believe that other planets have a larger wobble than Earth because they don't have a large moon like ours. For example, it has been discovered that Mars has a wobble that is more severe than Earth's.

The seasons of Earth are caused by its tilt as it orbits around the sun once every year. As the moon helps to stabilize the earth's wobble, it also helps to maintain our regular seasonal patterns that we all depend on.

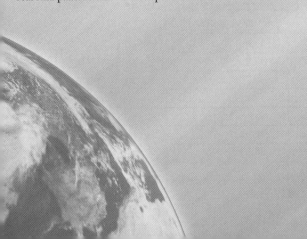

Gravity

What is gravity and what would we do without it?

Gravity is the tendency of masses to move toward one another. Sir Isaac Newton was the first to describe and define gravity. Why two objects have this attraction towards one another is still basically unknown. We just know that it happens and our lives depend on it. Many of the laws of physics depend on gravity.

If gravity here on Earth was less, our bones would not be as strong and our muscles would become weak. Astronauts who are weightless in space must do exercises to keep their muscles and bones healthy.

If you weighed 100 pounds on earth, you would weigh the following on the moon and other planets:

Planet	Weight (pounds)
Moon	16.6
Mercury	37.8
Venus	90.7
Mars	37.7
Jupiter	253.3
Saturn	106.4
Uranus	88.9
Neptune	112.5
Pluto	6.7

Use the table to answer the following questions:

Which planet would you weigh the least on?

Which planet would you weigh the most on?

Which planet has gravity that is the closest to the earth's gravity?

How much would you weigh on the planet that you would like to visit?

I weight only 20 lb!!

PLUTO

There are certain things that we need in order to live on earth:

Necessities for Human Life
Water
Oxygen
Light
Atmosphere
Suitable temperature
Food source

Use this list of necessities for human life to determine if you would be able to live on any of the other planets.

The Other Planets

Mercury
Has no air
Has no water
Temperature ranges from 800 degrees to 300
degrees below zero

Venus
Continuous thunder
Temperatures greater than 900 degrees
Carbon dioxide in its atmosphere
Acid clouds
Heavy atmospheric pressure

Mars
No air to breathe
Temperatures 100 degrees below zero

Jupiter
Bad weather- typhoon that has been happening for
300 years
No solid surface
Crushing air pressure
Cosmic radiation showers
Gases like methane and ammonia in the atmosphere

Saturn
Has no air

Uranus
Has a methane atmosphere

Neptune
Temperatures down to 328 degrees below zero

Pluto
It is so far from the sun that you would instantly freeze to death.

Other Moons

There are also many moons in our solar system, too many to talk about here, but here are a few interesting facts:

Janus and Epimetheus, two of Saturn's moons have close orbits. About every four years the moons catch up to one another, revolve around one another, and then trade orbits. Callisto, a moon of Jupiter, is the heaviest cratered moon in our solar system and Europa, is the smoothest. Yet, they both circle Jupiter. Finally, Io, a moon of Jupiter, is a small moon that may have active volcanoes on its surface.

The Earth is unique among all the planets

The earth has all of the qualities necessary for human life!

Its looks: The earth looks different than any other planet. From space, it shows the greens of the forests, the blues of the oceans, the browns of the mountains, and the whites of the glaciers.

Its position: The earth is in just the right spot in relation to the sun. If we were closer to the sun we would burn up and if we were farther from the sun we would freeze.

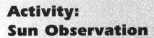

Activity:
Sun Observation

Materials

 Binoculars

Direct sunlight

Mirror

Procedure: Find a window or door that can be opened so direct sunlight shines in. Place the binoculars (set them on the window sill or wedge them in the door) so that the direct sunlight goes through at least one lens of the binoculars. Place a mirror in front of one of the eye pieces of the binoculars so that an image is projected on a wall of the room. Darken the room. You should be able to see an image of the sun on the wall. Adjust the mirror to focus the image. DO NOT look into the binoculars, or the directly into the mirror -- this could damage your eyes. Observe the sun on the wall. Draw a picture of the image that you see.

Did you know that each square inch of the sun's surface shines with the intensity of 300,000 candles?!

Its distance: The earth is just the right distance form the sun. The earth absorbs one billionth of the sun's power. This amount it just right for the living systems on earth and provides energy for plants, the water cycle, and other support systems here on Earth.

Its water: The ocean absorbs a large part of the sun's energy, and then releases it later when it gets cool. This keeps the earth from being too hot during the day and too cold at night.

Properties of water include: its ability to dissolve things such as minerals -- making salt water, its ability to expand and fill space, its surface tension, its ability to absorb heat, and it comes in three forms: liquid, solid, and gas (vapor).

Let's look more closely at the three forms of water.
Have you noticed that ice cubes in your cup float instead of sink? Why do you think that happens? To find the answer lets do another short experiment.

Experiment: Why does ice float?

Materials

Plastic container   Water   Freezer

Procedure: Fill the plastic container about an inch from the top with water. Use a waterproof marker to mark the water line on the container. Carefully place the container in the freezer with out spilling any. Let it freeze. When the water has frozen, take the container out and check to see where the top of the ice is in comparison with the mark you made earlier. Is the top of the ice above or below your mark? Why do you think that this happened? When frozen, water molecules actually expand. This creates space between the molecules causing the ice to float.

Why is it important for ice to float?

Imagine a lake filled with fish, plants and other animals. In the winter, ice forms on the top of the lake. What if the ice sank to the bottom? Then another layer of ice would form on the top of the lake and it would sink again. Eventually the lake would fill with ice, killing all the creatures living in it. The fact that ice floats protects the animals in the water below.

Imagine an ocean with ice caps that formed and also sank. Eventually the ocean in that area would fill with ice, and make it hard for sea-life. The fact that ice floats, allows the sun to melt it back into water. This helps to maintain the balance between the amount of water and ice.

Interestingly, most other liquids become heavy and sink when they are frozen. The Creator made water unique so that life is possible here on Earth!

Our Air

Air has some properties that are opposite of water.

- It sinks as it gets cooler.
- When it heats up, it floats upward into the atmosphere.
  This helps keep the earth cooler.
- The hot air in the atmosphere creates air currents.
  This circulates the good air in the atmosphere.

If air had the same properties as water, our Earth would not be a good place for life. God, in His all-knowing wisdom, made air and water the opposite in these respects!

Jonathan Park

Part 3

Earth's Moon

We have been talking about the planets and our earth. Let's look at something that is the closest celestial object to Earth-our moon. Two common questions about the moon are:

1. How old is it?
2. Where did it come from?

Scientists have used a method called radioisotope dating to date moon rocks. However, these dating methods are based on three assumptions.

What are assumptions?
Being able to identify assumptions is a basic step in critical thinking. Assumptions are underlying thoughts about an idea or even an action.

Example: In a Japanese culture, they sleep and sit on the floor. **The assumption is that the ground is clean.** In the United States, we build our beds off of the ground. **The assumption is that the ground is dirty**.

Observation: It is raining and there is sunshine at the same time. I can reasonably *assume* that there may be a rainbow somewhere in the sky.

Observation: I am using a ruler to measure the length of my foot. I have to *assume* that the ruler is accurate.

In order to illustrate the assumptions of isotope dating, let's look at a candle.

You walk into a room and observe a candle burning. For eight minutes you watch the candle burn and you wonder how long the candle has been burning.

This is a similar question to a scientist asking "how old is this rock?"

How could you figure out how long the candle had been burning?

You could observe how far down the candle burns in a certain amount of time. In order to do that you would have to guess the starting height of the candle. Then you would have to figure out how fast (the rate is) at which the candle is burning (you would do that by measuring the time that you have been an eye-witness).

How do you know if you are right? You have to make a few assumptions about the candle and its environment:

1. You must assume that the material of which the candle is made is consistent throughout the length of the candle:
   - The wax may be different, which affects its rate of burning.
   - The starting height of the candle is not known. You were not there at the beginning so your assumption may be wrong.

2. You must assume the rate of burning has always been constant or the same:
   - There are things that may make the candle burn faster. Maybe a gust of wind provided more oxygen in the room which would speed the burning. You were not there to see, so your assumption may be wrong.

3. You must assume that the candle has not been bothered by someone:
   - Someone may have blown out the candle for a period of time before relighting it. You have not observed the whole time the candle has been burning, so your assumption may be wrong.

The hard part is knowing if your assumptions are true. If not, then you will get a wrong answer.

Rocks are dated with similar assumptions. Rocks are made of several different elements such as lead or uranium. They are called isotopes and they decay or breakdown over long periods of time. This decay rate, like the candle burning, is what scientists measure to find the age of a rock.

The three assumptions are:
1. Known amounts of isotopes at the start.
2. Constant decay or breakdown rate.
3. Nothing was lost or added to the rock.

It is known that there are problems with these assumptions. They are similar to the assumptions you made about the burning candle. It is hard to tell the exact amounts of material in which the rock started. Also, there may have been major events in the earth's history that would affect the rate of decay. It is also reasonable that rocks could be contaminated or that they've lost some of their material. So, these dating assumptions may be incorrect, and therefore the radiometric way of dating rocks may be wrong.

The Race to the Moon

Moon exploration was a goal of the Soviet Union and the United States for many years. Because both countries were trying to be 'the first' it fueled the race to space and then on to the moon:

1957

October 4
U.S.S.R. launches Sputnik 1, the world's first artificial satellite.

1958

January 31
First U.S. artificial satellite, Explorer 1, launch is successful and it identifies Van Allen radiation belts.

April 2
President Eisenhower proposes NASA.

December 17
Project Mercury announced.

1959

January 2
Soviet satellite Luna 1 is the first to achieve earth-escape velocity, comes within 5,998 km of the Moon, and goes into solar orbit.

September 12
The Soviet Union launches Luna 2 which reaches its target on the moon by September 14th.

1960

August 10
Discoverer 13 becomes the first man-made object to be recovered from orbit.

August 19
Soviet Sputnik 5 is the first mission to return successful live cargo from space to Earth. After 17 orbits, the satellite returns the dogs Belka and Strelka and six mice.

ay 5

an B. Shepard Jr. is America's
st man in space in 1961. His
ercury Freedom 7 spacecraft,
ached an altitude of 116.5
les and traveled 303.8 miles
wn range, splashing down in
e ocean near the Bahamas.

ay 25

esident Kennedy announces
e goal of landing astronauts
the Moon before 1970.

ctober 27

rst Saturn rocket launch is a
ccess.

1962

February 20

John H. Glenn, Jr., becomes
the first American to orbit
the Earth in Friendship 7, a
2987-pound spacecraft.
Completed three orbits in
4.9 hours.

1964

October 12

The first three man crew in
space: Vladimir Komarov,
Konstantin Feoktistov and
Boris Yegorov, return after
16 orbits.

1965

March 23

The first manned flight of the
Gemini program (the second
wave of missions by NASA to get
man to the moon). Virgil I.
Grissom and John W. Young
orbited the Earth 3 times.''

June 3

Astronaut Edward H. White II is
the first American to "walk" in
space during the flight of Gemini
4. White floated out of the cockpit
and into space. While McDivitt
took photographs, White
"walked" for 21 minutes at the
end of his "umbilical cord." He
compared the experience to flying
over the Earth in an airplane.

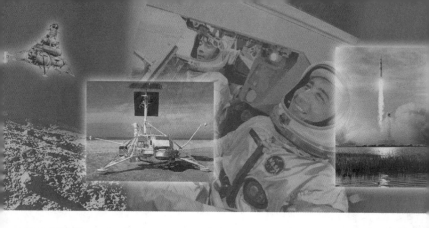

1966
January 31
The Soviet Union launches Luna 9 which makes the first soft landing on the Moon. The spacecraft returned photographs of the surface of the moon for three days.

May 30
The launch of the first U.S. spacecraft to make a soft landing on the moon. In almost six weeks of operation, it took 11,150 photographs.

1967
January 27
Apollo1 astronauts Virgil I. Grissom, Edward H. White II, and Roger B. Chaffee die when fire engulfed their Apollo command module during a ground test at Kennedy Space Center, Florida. The three were scheduled to fly the first manned Apollo mission. The tragedy caused the Apollo program to be delayed for months and resulted in many design modifications to the interior of the Apollo command module.

1968
Dec. 21-27
On Christmas Eve, the Apollo 8 crew are the first humans to orbit the Moon. The astronauts Frank Borman, James A. Lovell Jr., and William A. Anders lifted off at 7:51 a.m. (E.S.T.) on Dec. 21, 1968. They photographed the Moon during their 20-hour stay in lunar orbit and saw the Earth as a small, blue ball more than 381,404 kilometers (237,000 miles) away.

1969
July 16-24

As Apollo 11 pilot Michael Collins orbits the moon, Neil A. Armstrong radioed to Mission Control the familiar phrase, "The Eagle has landed!" On July 20, Armstrong and Edwin E. Aldrin Jr. take the first human steps on the moon. The astronauts stayed outside their lunar module for more than two hours and collected over 47 pounds of samples from the landing site in the Sea of Tranquility.

1970
September 12

The Soviet Union launches Luna 16. This automated lunar mission lands in the Moon's Sea of Fertility on September 20. It completed its mission to collect lunar soil samples and return to Earth on September 24.

1971
July 26-Aug. 7

The fourth U.S. lunar landing, Apollo 15, astronauts David R. Scott and James B. Irwin explore the moon's surface for over 18 hours in the roving vehicle. Pilot Alfred M. Worden conducted extensive photographic mapping from lunar orbit.

1972
April 16-27

Apollo 16 astronauts John W. Young, Thomas K. Mattingly II, and Charles M. Duke, Jr., photographed the Earth's auroras using special film sensitive to ultraviolet radiation. When they landed on the moon near the crater Descartes, Young and Duke explored the surface for over 20 hours, collecting 210.4 pounds of lunar samples. A space walk was also conducted by pilot Mattingly.

1973

July 28

On the Skylab 3 mission, a crew of three astronauts make it to the Skylab space station, and stayed there for 59 days.

1975

July 15

Three American astronauts and three Soviet cosmonauts participated together on a mission called the Apollo Soyuz Test Project (ASTP). Soyuz 19 and Apollo 18 dock on the 36th orbit of Soyuz, they remained in orbit together almost 6 days.

Moon Dust

When we reached the moon in 1969, it was the exciting event of the time. Many children throughout all of history have wondered about this mysterious world. One of the mysteries that the moon landing helped to answer was how much dust was on the surface, and how far the lunar module would sink into the surface of the moon.

Dust from space collects on all planets and moons throughout our solar system. Here on Earth that dust is cleaned-up by wind and rain. But on the moon, it just continues to collect. So the older the moon is -- the more dust we should find. Just prior to the Apollo program, the rate at which the dust collected was thought to be very high. So there was some concern that there might be so much dust, that the lunar module or astronauts may sink deep. But as we sent probes to the moon just before Apollo - like the Surveyor - we found that there was just a thin layer of dust. Many claimed that proved the moon was young.

The problem is that since that time there has been a big question about how fast the dust really does collect on the moon. Many scientists are now saying that it collects so slowly that the moon could be very old and still only have a thin layer. So, a thin layer of dust *may* indicate a young age for the moon. However, since we don't really know the rate at which the dust collects, we can't say for sure. So to be honest, we need to sit tight until we do know. In other words, for now the moon dust issue should be dropped by creationists until we get all the facts.

Life on the Moon?

The astronauts of the Apollo missions used to be quarantined or isolated from others just in case they brought back some strange bacteria from the moon. But by the Apollo 15 mission they were no longer concerned about life on the moon.

If there was life on the moon, where do you think it would have come from? Here are three possibilities:

1. First would be if it had evolved.

Science has proved that life can only come from life. We know that it is impossible for life to spontaneously start on a totally dead moon like ours. Evolution has never been proven - and it goes against the Bible.

2. Second, maybe God could've created the moon with life already on it.

There doesn't seem to be anything in the Bible that mentions God creating life anywhere else. And everything that we've observed on the moon has shown that there's no life there. And so both the Bible and science seem to point to no life on the moon.

3. Or finally, maybe microbes could've traveled from Earth to the moon with the spaceship or on the astronauts.

However, they never found that anything had been transferred to the moon from Earth. So there hasn't been any life found on our moon, and it seems as if the same thing goes for all other planets and moons throughout our universe. It really seems that Earth is the only place in which life exists.

The Apollo Hoax

Did we really land on the moon? There are some people who believe that it was all a hoax! They claim that they have evidence that the moon missions were faked. They say that there are problems with the video and pictures transmitted back from the Apollo Missions:

1. Unparallel shadows

Problem: In some photos, objects appear to make shadows in unparallel directions. They suggest that there is more than one source of light besides the sun, which could be evidence that they faked the images in a Hollywood studio.

Answer: Objects on a flat surface will cast parallel shadows, but the Moon's surface is bumpy and uneven. Because of the different angles of the ground, shadows were cast in unparallel directions.

2. Rock with a "C"

Problem: A picture taken from Apollo 16 moon landing shows a rock with a letter 'C' on it. Some would say that this rock was a prop that had a label that was supposed to be removed before filming. It really does appear to be a letter 'C'.

Answer: When the original negatives of the picture were looked at, there was not a letter 'C' on the rock. It seems that something was accidentally added when the film was developed later.

3. Flag waving

Problem: In many photos it appears that the flag is waving as if being blown by the wind. But there is no atmosphere on the moon to cause the flag to wave. So the picture must be a fake.

Answer: It is known that there is a horizontal bar in which the flag was attached. Astronauts Aldrin and Armstrong had trouble extending the bar out as far as it could go, so they left it that way. This created creases in the material of the flag, making it look like it is actually waving. It then became a tradition of the Apollo missions to not fully extend the flag.

4. Who filmed Armstrong as he stepped out onto the moon?

Problem: The event of Neil Armstrong stepping out onto the moon was broadcast on television so that all could witness the event. However, if Armstrong was the first man on the moon, who was shooting the camera? It must be a fraud.

Answer: NASA engineers built a video camera onto the outside of the Lunar Module. Aldrin, the man inside the module turned on the camera and Armstrong pulled it into position, thus not needing a cameraman to film the event.

5. Lit astronaut in dark shadows

Problem: Several photos show an astronaut standing in the shadow of the Lunar Module, but you can clearly see the astronaut. Some say that this means there must have been another light source shining on him.

Answer: The surface of the moon is very reflective, like the snow reflecting the sun. In a sense there are two light sources; the sun and the light reflecting off the moon's surface. Because the astronauts were wearing white suits the reflective light from the moon's surface was enough to illuminate their suits making them visible in the shadows.

Nothing Left to Chance

According to evolution, the origin of life was left to chance.

What if NASA worked in that way? However, they left nothing to chance when sending man to the moon. They used operational science to plan every aspect of the flights. Operational or observational science is the type of science that invents technology, does experiments to solve problems, and makes medicines to help people.

Origin science – the study of beginnings – is a different type of science. This is the debate about evolution and creation. Since no one was around to see the beginning of this universe, scientists have to look at the evidence to decide how they think our world began. Evolution leaves the beginning of life to chance. However, in the Bible, we learn that God is the Creator!

Romans 1:21 says *"Because that, when they knew God, they glorified him not as God, neither were thankful; but became vain in their imaginations, and their foolish heart was darkened."*

Most scientists recognize the wonder, complexity, and beauty of creation yet choose to give all the credit to evolution. How can all those scientists be wrong? This is a hard question. In Romans it tells us that their imaginations were vain and their hearts were darkened to the truth. They are blinded to what may seem obvious to us- that God is creator of the universe!

Created Kinds

Do you have a favorite animal? Why is it your favorite?

Genesis 1:21 & 25 gives us six categories of animals that God created during the week of creation:

Great whales ○

Every creature that moves in the water ○

Winged fowl ○

Cattle ○

Beast ○

Everything that creeps along the ground ○

Draw a line matching a category from the left with the animals on the right.

Which category does your favorite animal fit into?

Materials:

Pencil or pen

A piece of paper

Instructions:

Write the name of the six categories that God created at the top of the paper. List the names of every animal that you can think of that would fit in each category. You should be able to fill the page with all types of animals.

Did you remember spiders, clams, and dinosaurs? Don't forget that just because dinosaurs may not be alive today, God still created them.

Into what category would dinosaurs fit? They could fit into beasts, winged birds (Pterodactyls), and even great sea creatures (Plesiosaur).

Unfossilized Dinosaur

Parts

Many people are very interested in the dinosaur T-rex. Its full name is Tyrannosaurus Rex. T-rex can be 20 ft long, 50 ft tall, and weigh 6 or 7 tons. Its skull is about 6 ft long. It has a 24 inch foot print and its front fang is 7 inches long. Its brain, however, was only about the size of its front fang.

Dinosaur Fossils May Not Be as Old as Some People Think.

In 1990, people at Montana State University found an almost complete T-rex fossil. Amazingly, some unfossilized red blood cells were found in one of its legs!! This means that the fossil may not be as old as evolution claims.

In 2005, a T-rex fossil was being transported. They had to break one of its thigh bones in order to make it transportable. Again, they found soft, unfos- silized tissue inside the dinosaur's bone.

After these two discoveries, Dr. Mary Schweitzer, from Montana State University, found soft tissue in a Hadrosaur. Hadrosaurs are duck bill dinosaurs that are found in North America and China. The soft tissue that she found was like bone collagen of modern specimens.

This evidence challenges evolution's theory that the fossils are 65 million years old. How could soft tissues and blood cells remain soft for that long? Before this discovery, evolutionists had said that soft tissue could only last one hundred thousand years. This evidence suggests that dinosaurs only lived thousands of years ago, NOT millions.

Variation in Animals

There is often confusion when adaptation and evolution are talked about so let's define some terms.

Macro-evolution

is large scale changes in an animal – change from one kind into another kind. An Example would be a fish changing to become a frog or an ape becoming a human. *This type of evolution has never been observed.*

Micro-evolution

is small changes in an animal that allow it to adapt to its environment. An example of this would be a change in hair color or length. The proper term for this is not evolution but adaptation. *This can be observed in animals all the time.*

Example: Picture a group of mice that live in a field. The field is a dark brown color. The mice that live in the field are mostly a dark brown color, though there are some light brown mice. The lighter colored mice usually get eaten first by predators. Over time, the field begins to change color to a light brown or blonde color. The dark brown mice are very easily seen by predators and they would be eaten first because they do not blend into their surroundings. The blonde mice are now better adapted to life in the blonde colored field.

How do these changes come about?

This is where the disagreement between evolution and creation comes into play.

Evolution says that a mutation has occurred in the DNA of the field mouse. Mutations are mistakes and accidents. The mistake changed the mouse's color, allowing it to adapt.

How can an accidental mistake make life better for a mouse? Mathematically it is very, very, unlikely. In fact, mutations almost always create a bad result rather than a helpful change.

Creation says that this change was already programmed into the DNA and it allowed the mouse to change color to ensure its survival in its changing environment.

Again, you can see the theme of evolution--accidents and random chance happenings and the theme of creation--purposeful design.

Let's look at Genesis, Chapter 1:21 & 25:

"21And God created great whales, and every living creature that moveth, which the waters brought forth abundantly, after their kind, and every winged fowl after his kind: and God saw that it was good."

"25And God made the beast of the earth after his kind, and cattle after their kind, and every thing that creepeth upon the earth after his kind: and God saw that it was good."

From these verses you can see the categories of animals that God created which we talked about earlier. There is also something else that is important -- the word 'kind'.

How many times is the word 'kind' used?

The word 'kind' gives us a clue to how God may have designed animals. The fact that the word is repeated several times means that it is important. Kind can mean a type of animal. Notice that animals can only reproduce animals of their own kind -- not any other kind. This means that dogs reproduce only dogs. A dog never reproduces a cat. Dogs and cats are different kinds. People and apes are different kinds. Frogs and lizards are different kinds.

The animal kinds are able to survive and adapt to their surroundings because of the design of their genetic material, DNA. As we learned on page 48, our genetic material has genes that are dominate and recessive. There are genes that are hidden because they are covered up by another gene. Only under the right circumstances would a hidden gene be seen. This is natural variation that is already designed inside the genetic material of a kind of animal.

There can be many variations of hair color or size within the same animal kind which allows it to survive in its special environment. Another example of this is a kind of Manchurian Hare (rabbit). One hare is best adapted to life in the forest and another is best adapted to life in the meadow next to the forest. The forest hare and the meadow hare have breed to form new a hare that is best suited for the boundary in-between of the forest and meadow.

> **Each of these three hares is adapted to their special habitat. They are three variations of one kind of animal!**

Most likely, when God created the animals He did not create the exact colors, sizes, and variations that we see today, but He created the original kinds. An original pair of animals had offspring that have varied throughout the centuries.

You may have heard the word 'species' in science class. Do not confuse 'species' and 'kind'. A kind is not equal to species. A species can be a variation within a kind of animal. For example, several different species of monkeys have actually been traced back to the same monkey "kind".

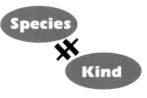

Design of a Snowflake

Each snowflake is unique -- there are no two flakes that look the same, and each is a marvel of beauty in and of itself.

The white color of snow reflects some sunlight back into space. This keeps the snow cooler and helps keep the earth cooler. God uses snow to maintain the balance of temperatures here on earth.

Keeping the snow cool is important because it stores much of the water that the earth needs during the rainless seasons. God has designed snow to hold that water, and then release it later when it melts.

Water stored as snow protects the earth from the massive erosion that would take place if it all fell as rain. The rushing waters would eat away at soil, and sweep away plants.

Snow acts as a protective blanket for the plants and seeds that it covers during the cold winter months.

Koch Snowflake Activity

Materials:

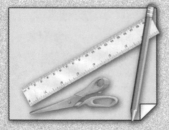

White piece of standard paper

Pencil

Ruler

Scissors

Procedure:

In the center of the paper, using a pencil and ruler, draw an equilateral triangle (having three equal sides) with sides measuring 12cm each. On each side of the triangle, make a mark at 4cm and 8cm. Next, draw another equilateral using the line between the 4cm and 8cm marks as the base. You will now have three new triangles poking out from the sides and base of the original triangle making a six pointed star shape. On each side of the new triangles make marks at the 1.3 and 2.7cm measures. Make twelve new equilateral triangles. Continue. See diagram.

Koch snowflake diagram

Now you can cut out your snowflake and hang it up on your refrigerator, or decorate your room!

From the snowflake activity you can see the design of just one snowflake. Think of all the variations that you could have made. When God made snow, He made it so each flake is different. Animals also have design features that make them unique and specially suited for the habitat that they live in. It is easy to see that God had it all figured out!

Part 2

Salmon are Very Interesting and Unique Fish.

Have you ever seen a salmon?

Where do salmon live?

Do salmon live in more than one place during their lives?

Are these fish important to people? Why?

The Life of a Salmon

In the season of Autumn, salmon lay their eggs in the gravel of the bottom of rivers and streams on the west coast of the United States and Canada. They burry these eggs one to two feet deep.

When the eggs hatch they are called alevins (sac fry). They stay buried in the gravel for a few more weeks and they have a yolk sac attached to them that supplies their food.

When the salmon emerges from the gravel, it is called a fry. They swim to protected areas like a deep pool, around tree roots, undercut river banks, and submerged logs. In these areas, fry eat insects and other small water creatures. They stay in the protected area for several months and gradually grow to be able to swim in swifter currents.

The next stage is called smolts. It is in this stage that they begin to journey downstream towards the ocean. An amazing transformation takes place when they swim downstream. Just before they enter the ocean, there is an area that is called an estuary. An estuary is the place where fresh and salt water meets. It is sometimes called brackish water. The smolt adapts from being a freshwater fish to a saltwater fish! Often the smolt will stay in the estuary adjusting to the salt and growing larger with new things to eat.

Adult salmon swim around the ocean for two to four years. They grow very large.

Near the end of a salmon's life when it is time to lays eggs or spawn, it journeys back to the place it started life.

How do you think that the salmon knows how to find the river of its own birth?

Scientists think that the fish may be able to smell or taste their own river. Scientists also think that it may have something to do with the position of the sun, moon, and stars, and the earth's magnetic field. This is a remarkable ability for the fish to recognize its home.

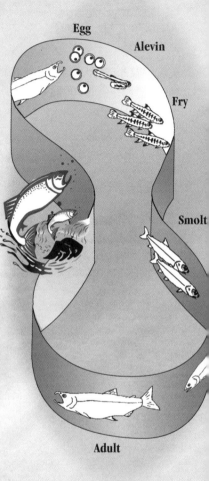

Lifecycle of a salmon

Before going back up the river, the salmon has to adjust to the fresh water again. Most of them at this point also stop eating. There are many obstacles that the salmon has to swim over, around, or through to make it to its final place.

Chinook salmon are large fish so they lay their eggs in larger gravel. Steelhead are smaller so they lay their eggs in smaller gravel. This ensures that everyone has a place to lay their precious eggs. A female salmon finds a mate and digs a deep hole with her tail and lays her eggs. Then the male salmon fertilizes the eggs and the cycle repeats.

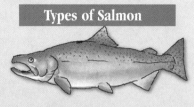

Chinook or King

Pink or Humpy

Silver or Coho

Sockeye or Red

Chum

Atlantic salmon or **steelhead** is often listed but are ocean going rainbow trout.

The salmon's life is quite an incredible journey. Yet every year it happens again and again according to an amazing plan. Do you think that God was involved with planning of the lifecycle of the salmon?

Male polar bears can weigh 775-1500 pounds. They are very large bears.

What makes a polar bear unique from other bears?

One thing that makes it unique is its color -- or you could say lack of color. They have two types of hair. Wool-like hair close to the skin to keep it warm and the long, hollow transparent hair that makes the polar bear white. The polar bear's hair appears white because it does not have colored pigment in it -- it is clear. Because of this special property, the hair reflects light helping to blend into the snow.

A strange thing happened in 1979. Three polar bears in the San Diego Zoo turned green! They discovered that there were colonies of green algae living in the hollow hair of the bears. They got rid of the algae by giving them a special bath.

Polar bears have a layer of blubber that is 4 inches thick. This layer keeps them warm and helps them to be able to float when they are swimming. They also have special webbed paws that enable them to swim 4-6 miles per hour.

Caribou are similar to elk but have some special design features that make them unique. These features involve their hoofs, hair, and running ability. Just as Polar bears have special webbed feet to help them swim better, Caribou also have special hooves to help them swim!

Concaved hoofs- concaved means curved inward. The hoofs are curved in a way that helps them to paddle when they swim and helps them to walk in the deep snow better so that they don't sink down as far.

Hair-They have hollow hair that actually makes them lighter when they swim.

Running ability- they have great speed and can run up to 50 mph.

Have you ever seen a porcupine in real life? They are interesting and cute animals. They can be found in North America, part of Central America, and Africa. In North America, they grow to a length of 2-3 feet long (including tail) and have about 30,000 spines or quills. In Africa, porcupines are much larger and have huge quills that can be a foot long and 1/4 inch in diameter. That is the thickness of your pinky finger!

Porcupines have three types of hair:

A wooly undercoat for warmth

A coat of long hair for insulation

A unique hair called spines or quills

Porcupine self-defense:

They will run into an enemy with their quills or slap them with their tail. The quills are designed with small barbs that spread out when they enter the body of an enemy. The barbs also move the quill deeper into the skin as the animal moves around- nearly an inch a day.

"Ouch" says the porcupine, "I have been stuck by my own quill." This can happen often to a porcupine, but amazingly, the tips of its quills have an antibiotic that fights infection. The Creator thought of everything!

Porcupines don't see very well but they have a very strong sense of smell and use their whiskers to guide them. Their long claws help them climb trees. This process of climbing trees strips bark and limbs and this feeds other animals that live on the ground.

Dogs are a great example of the variation possible within one kind of animal.

It is known that wolves are the originators of domestic dogs. There is debate as to how many years ago that people began to breed wolves in order to domesticate dogs. Some scientists say that there was an original wolf stock that God created. This theory of one wolf stock has come from DNA comparisons and could fit a biblical model.

The North American wolf is ancestor to the Eskimo Dog

The Chinese wolf is ancestor to Chows, Toy spaniels and Pekinese breeds

The Indian wolf is ancestor to a large group which includes Greyhounds and Salukis

The European wolf is ancestor to Sheep dogs, Terriors, and related breeds

Dogs vary extremely in size, color, and personality.

The smallest dog breed is the Chihuahua with a height of 6-8 inches. It may have originated in South America. There is historical evidence traced to the Aztec and Toltec civilizations.

The tallest dog breed is the Irish Wolfhound with a height of 35 inches-that is nearly three feet tall. It originated in Ireland and was used for hunting and battle.

Pomeranians can make good companions, English sheepdogs can herd animals, Bloodhounds are good hunters, Dalmatians can help us do work, Labrador Retrievers can be trained as seeing eye dogs, and Rottweillers can be trained to do police work.

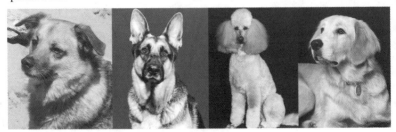

There is so much variety when it comes to dogs!

Can you use your own words to describe what the idea of "lots of variety" means?

With all this variety do you see any dogs that are becoming some other kind of animal?

No, the variety just makes more interesting dogs.

Not all animals have such a wonderful variety (think of an alligator, they don't have as many varieties as dogs). All animals have a natural variation boundary that God designed within their DNA. For some animals, it is a wide variety, and for others it's much smaller. This boundary makes sure that a dog remains a dog, and a cat remains a cat.

Boundaries are an important part of life for animals and humans. Those boundaries provide for us and protect us.

Wilderness Express Crossword Puzzle

Across

2. Another name for a King salmon.
4. Dinosaurs may __ be as old as some people think
5. Something that makes polar bears' paws unique from other bears.
8. The smallest dog breed.
10. Another word for micro-evolution.
11. True or False-unfossilized dinosaur parts have been found.
12. Length of a T-Rex's front fang (in inches).
13. There are ___ different categories of created animals.

Down

1. The stage when salmon begin to journey downstream.
3. A word for the Biblical concept that is similar to species.
6. Something that God gave animals and humans to provide and protect.
7. There are many ___ of dogs.
9. A country where hadrosaurs are found.

Solution:

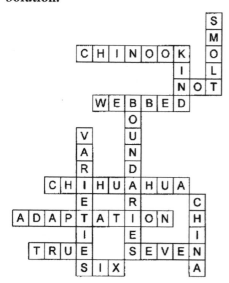